THE MAGICAL MISADVENTURES OF
Prunella Bogthistle

THE MAGICAL MISADVENTURES OF
Prunella Bogthistle

DEVA FAGAN

Henry Holt and Company ✹ New York

I owe enormous thanks to R. J. Anderson, Melissa Caruso, Megan Crewe, Troy Danko, Justin Hughes, Hope Ring, Charles Schweppe, Pamela Seltsam, and E. Catherine Tobler for reading various incarnations of this book and providing feedback. I am especially grateful to Geoffrey Bottone, who went above and beyond the call of duty to help me stay sane when I was bogged down in a particularly thorny rewrite. Many thanks as well to Kevin Hamor and everyone involved in Grimwode for their roles in the genesis of Prunella and Barnaby.

I will be forever grateful to my agent, Shawna McCarthy, for being tough on me when I needed her to be, and for sticking with this book through the downs and the ups.

Many, many thanks to my wonderful editor, Reka Simonsen, for her wise insights and sharp eyes, and to the entire Holt production team for their efforts on behalf of this book.

Lastly, thank you to the friends and family who encouraged me during the writing of this book, especially my husband, Bob, who provided endless enthusiasm and optimism, and who trusted me to give Barnaby a good home.

Henry Holt and Company, LLC, *Publishers since 1866*

175 Fifth Avenue, New York, New York 10010

www.HenryHoltKids.com

Henry Holt® is a registered trademark of Henry Holt and Company, LLC.

Text copyright © 2010 by Deva Fagan

All rights reserved.

Distributed in Canada by H. B. Fenn and Company Ltd.

Library of Congress Cataloging-in-Publication Data

Fagan, Deva.

The magical misadventures of Prunella Bogthistle / Deva Fagan.—1st ed.

p.   cm.

Summary: The personal quests of a young witch who aspires to be a villain and a young thief who is determined to become a hero intersect in a swampy bog.

ISBN 978-0-8050-8743-7

[1. Magic—Fiction. 2. Witches—Fiction. 3. Heroes—Fiction.

4. Blessing and cursing—Fiction.] I. Title.

PZ7.F136Mag 2010   [E]—dc22   2009023447

First Edition—2010 / Book designed by Véronique Lefèvre Sweet

Printed in April 2010 in the United States of America by

R.R. Donnelley & Sons Company, Harrisonburg, Virginia

1   3   5   7   9   10   8   6   4   2

To my parents,
Paul and Cynthia,
for their love, inspiration,
and steadfast support

THE MAGICAL MISADVENTURES OF
Prunella Bogthistle

Chapter 1

All I wanted was to charm a single stinking wart onto my face. Yes, onto, not off. A good bog-witch should have at least one. Grandmother had eleven, and a hooked nose to boot. Of course, there were rare witches who could pull off a certain dark and terrible beauty. My mother was one, according to Grandmother. Maybe that's how I got stuck the way I was.

I peered into the moon-silvered water of the rain barrel. No wart. No dark and terrible beauty, either. Just the same clear brown skin and snub nose I'd always had. Blast it! I smacked my palm into the water. A true bog-witch wouldn't be sniffling, I told myself fiercely. This only made the tears slip faster down my cheeks. Because I wasn't a true bog-witch; everyone from Grandmother to my littlest cousin, Ezzie, knew it. That was why they were all off on a midnight mushroom spree, and I was stuck here, alone, keeping watch over Grandmother's garden.

I blinked up at the moon. If I closed my eyes, I could almost see them: my cousins, my aunts, my great-aunts, my second cousins twice removed. All of them out there under that brilliant silver eye, laughing and teasing and dancing. I could almost smell the sweet wood-smoke, taste the earthy, buttery fried mushrooms. I loved fried mushrooms. But more than that, I loved being a Bog-thistle witch. Even if no one else thought I was one, really.

It wasn't fair. I could twitch a fire out of soggy twigs as well as any of them. I could charm away Ezzie's winter sniffles. Grandmother herself admitted that she couldn't tell where I'd mended the chips in her best tea set. But those were still just baby spells. Until I proved myself with a proper curse, I would never be considered a true Bogthistle. And my curses, well, they just never turned out quite right.

I cringed, remembering the last one. The mob of Uplanders had descended on us on the eve of the full moon, jabbing the sharp tines of their pitchforks against the night. Their angry shouting drowned the fluting of the peepers. Their smoky torches burned the sweetness of the moonflowers from the air.

But we bog-witches were no strangers to mobs. Our

foremothers had settled their cozy collection of cottages smack in the middle of the bog for a reason. The sucking mire and stinging thistles kept the fools at bay long enough for us to puzzle out some sense from their furious bellows.

"We didn't steal the Mirable Chalice, you fool," Grandmother called over our spiny ramparts, her eyes blazing—really blazing, with green flames. I always wanted to learn that charm. "We've all the magic we could want here in the Bottomlands. What do we need with some Uplander bauble? Go take your torches and burn down the Mistveil Bayou if you want someone to blame. If anyone stole the chalice, it was that villain Blackthorn."

The mob gave a rabblesome roar, sprinkled with shouts of "Foul hags!" and "Burn them all!" One particularly mouthy fellow at the front called out, "You stole the chalice, you harpies! You brought this curse to our lands! Our corn withers and dies, our children sicken, our homes crumble. We're here to put a stop to it!" He waved his torch at the wall of thistles. "Give it back, or we'll burn this place to the ground!"

Grandmother's nostrils flared. She drew herself even taller, like a great thunderhead about to loose a torrent of lightning. A few yelps and yips rose from the Uplanders. Even the mouthy fellow stepped back.

"So—a bit of trouble with your corn and you think you're cursed? It's time you learned the misery and woe of a *true* bog-witch curse."

That was when she'd looked at me. I smothered a yelp of my own.

"Prunella," Grandmother commanded, "even you ought to be able to find a suitable punishment for these ignorant lunatics."

I thought I had just the curse. I thought that was my chance to show my true bog-witchery, to prove myself. A rain of alligator spoor *sounded* perfectly horrible. And in my defense, it did chase them hooting and hollering out of the mire and back to their Upland homes. How was I to know it would settle over their land and give them the best harvest in ages?

They had fields full of golden ears within two weeks. By the third, they were showing up on the outskirts of the bog, begging for more charms to stop crumbling chimneys and heal fevers and coughs. They trampled the mushroom patch and scared away all the nesting herons with their hubbub. In the end, Grandmother had to curse three of them with pustulous boils just to get them to leave us alone. And it was all my fault.

So that's how I ended up stuck in the garden, alone. Grandmother's garden didn't need watching. It was warded and trapped to the gills, tighter than the queen's treasure house. And who would want to steal her beans and pumpkins in any case? Someone would have to be an idiot, or desperate, or both, to try. Yet here I was, with only the fluting of the frogs and the twinkle of fireflies for company. The truth was, my family didn't want me around. I was an embarrassment. Another tear slipped down my nose.

I needed more than just a wart. I needed a curse as fearsome and powerful as those of Esmeralda herself, the first, and greatest, Bogthistle. Even Grandmother spoke reverently about Esmeralda and her lost magics. Every night after dinner she led all the clan (except me, of course, since she said I'd spoil it) in cursing Lord Blackthorn, who stole Esmeralda's grimoire ages ago. Sometimes I dreamed of running off and finding that grimoire, and all her long-lost magics with it. Surely with a book like that even I could learn to curse properly. Then I'd lead the mushroom sprees. Then I'd be taught the deepest Bogthistle secrets. Grandmother might even smile at me, once. I'd caught her smiling at Ezzie, so I knew she did, sometimes. Just never at me.

It was a silly dream. Lord Blackthorn's manor was charmed up as tight as Grandmother's garden. And anyway, a true bog-witch wouldn't be glooming around wishing on stars. I raised my chin, pushing myself up. I might as well try the wart charm again. I had nothing better to do.

Creeeak. I stood still, sure I must be imagining things. No one could possibly have gotten into the garden without triggering one of the wards. But I knew the squeak of the alchemy-shop door all too well. It was what had given me away last week, when I tried to sneak in and listen to Grandmother teaching Ezzie how to turn herself into a crow.

"Thief!" I cried out, as I laid my hand on the pumpkin vine beside me, muttering my invocation. The green fronds hissed forward like serpents, coiling around the dark shadow that lurked beside the door.

The shadow grunted. I darted forward, my heart hammering a jubilant beat. I had done something right, finally. I'd caught a thief. Now, *that* ought to make Grandmother smile.

A cloud shifted. I crooked my finger. My curse had to work this time. The honor of the Bogthistles demanded it. Wan moonlight outlined the thief's features. It was a boy. The shock of it froze my bent finger in midair, jabbing out at him.

It wasn't that I'd never seen boys before. There were a few things we just couldn't get in the Bottomlands, and Grandmother could not do without her daily helping of licorice. I had been to the nearest town of Withywatch four times, trotting along after Grandmother as she did her shopping, both of us cowled and cloaked against prying eyes.

I'd watched straggly farmer boys goggling at me from their hay-heaped wagons. I'd beheld snappy city boys scrumming and playing like a pack of young hounds. Frankly, I hadn't seen what I was missing by living out in the bog. Yet something about this boy now standing in front of me made me hesitate.

He pushed back a fringe of honey-brown hair, looking fine and proud and determined. "Go on and curse me, bog-witch."

The words of the spell scrambled against my throat. He'd called me a bog-witch. He knew what I was! In that moment, I didn't care that he was glaring at me. If it weren't an entirely unwitchly thing to do, I would have flung my arms around his neck and danced with him under the moonlight.

"Well?" he said after a moment. "Are you going to stand there posing, or are you going to get it over with? I'm three inches deep in mud here."

I smothered my smile. "I'm just deciding on the best punishment for a thief."

"I'm not here to steal anything," he said, scowling.

"Oh? You sneak into bog-witch gardens for fun, do you?"

"I'm . . . I'm on a quest." He raised his chin slightly. "For the Mirable Chalice."

I rolled my eyes. "Oh, and of course we must be the ones who took it. Just like we're the ones to blame for every cough, storm, and broken wheelbarrow in the Uplands."

"You bog-witches tried to steal it once already," said the boy, crossing his arms. "Everyone knows that story."

"That was two hundred years ago!" I protested. "Besides, Esmeralda never wanted the chalice. She was trying to help you stupid Uplanders. And what thanks did she get? Chased off into the bog by a pack of ignorant goons!"

He shrugged. "So a few Uplanders think you stole the chalice. What's it matter to you? Seems to me you lot settled yourselves nice enough, if you don't mind the mud and muck." He gestured around at the garden. Something fluttered in his hand.

"What's that?" I saw a flash of purple checks as he tucked it behind his back. "That's one of my aunt's best dishtowels! Give that back!"

"Fine, fine. Don't get yourself in a twist." The boy tossed the wad of cloth at me. "I was just . . . borrowing it. A fellow needs to keep his hands clean. This place is filthy."

"If you don't like mud, you should have stayed in the Uplands, where you belong." I crossed my arms. "But you'd better learn to like it, seeing as I'm about to turn you into a frog."

"You can't do that," he protested. "I need to bring back the chalice. The whole of the Uplands is cursed."

"Oh, so you're some sort of hero, are you? Going to save the Uplands?"

His cocky air faltered, just for a moment. "Something like that."

"How did you even get in here?" I demanded. "Grandmother's wards and traps are the best in the land. Better than the queen's."

The boy leaned against the door. "Pff. It wasn't *that* hard."

How dare he look so nonchalant with pumpkin vines wound around his feet and a bog-witch about to curse him? Being a frog was too good for him. I clenched my teeth, trying to remember Grandmother's pustulous-boils curse.

"The squealer over by the cabbages was a good one," he added. "Nearly got me. You might have noticed if you weren't so busy with your beauty charms."

"Beauty charms?" I roared. "That's it!"

For an instant, in the flash of greenish light, I could see his fear. Why did it make my insides wither like a bit of old fish-bait? I faltered, stumbling over the invocation.

Suddenly he was moving, slithering free from the vines. The next moment, he had ducked behind one of the giant pumpkins. I ran forward to the limp green fronds he left behind. How had he gotten free? Had he cut them?

"Ugh!" I snatched back my hand, covered in something slimy and slippery. "What did you do?"

"Don't blame me," came his voice from somewhere among the gourds. He sounded annoyed. "I didn't ask you to douse me in oil. Though it sure did make it easy to slip free. I don't suppose you'd give me that rag back?"

"Oooo!" I tried to slow my hammering heart. I was not going to let myself get riled up by a straggly snot of a boy. "It was supposed to be *boils*, not *oils*!"

"If it makes you happy, you did ruin my favorite jacket," he said. "But I'll take that over boils any day. And now I think I'll leave you to your cabbages and your beauty charms. Though, if you ask me, you don't need them. You're pretty enough already. For a bog-witch." I caught the flash of his grin before he slipped away, deeper into the garden.

I opened my mouth, but I didn't have a curse strong enough. Then the asparagus fronds rustled. Oh no.

"Stop!" I cried.

"I'm not sticking around to see—"

"There's a spirit-rending ward in the asparagus bed!"

The rustling stopped.

Why was I helping him? He deserved— No, blast it, he didn't deserve to die. I knew that asparagus ward was Grandmother's best and most terrible. Asparagus is her favorite. She doesn't let anyone else have any, not even Ezzie.

I licked my lips, forcing the words out. "Did you . . . did you already step on the crooked root?"

"I'm standing on it now." His bravado couldn't entirely cover the shiver of fear in his voice. Good. At least he believed me.

"Don't move. If you step off it, the ward will trigger. Do you see something that looks like a big white stone?"

"Yes . . . eagh . . . that's not a stone."

"Crow skull," I said, making my way gingerly through the pumpkin patch. I didn't dare go much closer. Grandmother's traps would get me as easily as they'd get the boy. "You'll have to turn it round. So it's not watching the root. But carefully! If you jiggle it, you'll set it off."

"Don't worry, I can handle that."

"I'm not worried. It would serve you right to get your spirit obliterated."

"Then why are you helping me?"

I was asking myself the same question. Bog-witches didn't go around helping people, not unless they got something out of it.

I still had no answer a moment later, when he strolled out from the asparagus bed, a single green spear clamped between his teeth. He snapped off the tip. "Not bad," he said, crunching the mouthful. His boots squelched slightly as he stepped toward me. "Thanks for the warning. That was a spiffing good trap. I—well, of course I would have been fine, but, still, thanks. My name's Barnaby, by the way." He stuck out his hand.

I don't know what I would have done. My fingers shook. Half of me wanted to reach out and take his hand, while the other half still wanted to turn him into a frog. But I never found out, because that's when Grandmother came back.

She swept out from the night with her robes crackling. "Prunella!" she thundered. "What is this disgrace? I leave you to watch my garden and return to find you consorting with an Uplander?"

The force of her anger pressed me back. Blast it, I was cowering. I couldn't help it. "Grandmother, I—"

She seized fistfuls of air, as if prepared to tear the

night in two. "If you can't keep the garden safe for one evening, how do you expect to become one of us?"

"I *am* a Bogthistle," I said, trying to ignore the shivers racing through me. Stinking sloughs, I could not cry in front of her. That would doom me forever. "Please, I just need another chance."

"Please? *Please?* When does a Bogthistle ever use that polite twaddle?" She swatted my hands aside. "What Bogthistle would free a thief rather than cursing him?"

"It wasn't her fault," said the boy, with considerably more gumption than I would have expected, even from him. "She did curse me. Sort of . . . I mean, look at this jacket. It'll never be the same."

I wanted to wring his neck and hug him at the same time.

"That's quite enough out of you, boy," said Grandmother. She crossed her arms, her elbows poking out sharply. "I've given you chances, Prunella. I wanted to see you succeed. But it's clear as cloudless skies that you just aren't one of us."

"I *am* a Bogthistle—you'll see." I whirled on Barnaby, crooking my finger. His eyes widened.

"Hey!" He took a step back. "I thought you were helping me."

"Bogthistles don't help stupid Uplanders who waltz

into places they don't belong," I said, trying to sound as sharp and iron-hard as Grandmother. The boy would have a good life as a frog, I told myself. Much better than if I cursed him with the doom of a hundred misfortunes. I spat out the words, squinching my eyes at the end. I couldn't watch.

Brightness flared against my eyelids. But when I opened them, there was no frog. Only Barnaby, quirking a brow at me. "Was that supposed to be a curse?" He dusted off his jacket. "I reckon you'd better stick with the oil-dousing. All that did was give me spots in my eyes. Nice and flashy, though."

I sputtered, turning to Grandmother. "It's not fair. How can I prove I'm one of you when you won't tell me what to do?"

She didn't speak. Her look was enough. Never before had I seen sorrow in her eyes. I could stand Grandmother's anger. I could endure her chivvying over my failed curses. But I could not bear that look. The stern line of her lips trembled, just for a moment. I had to fix this.

"Pl— I mean, just tell me what you want, Grandmother. I'll do it."

The flash of sorrow was gone as if it had never been. She cocked her head, staring at me. "It's not a matter of what I want. What do *you* want, Prunella?"

"To be a proper Bogthistle." I scrambled for the words to convince her. "Just give me one more chance." I kept my knees locked in place, lest I fall to the muddy earth.

Grandmother huffed. She turned upon Barnaby. "It's your lucky day, asparagus thief. I won't turn you into a frog."

"Aahh . . . thank you?" Barnaby stepped back a pace anyway.

"You won't?" I asked.

"No. I'll leave that for you, Prunella. If you some-how manage to properly curse this thief—or anyone, for that matter—I just might reconsider things."

I rocked on my stiff legs, steadying myself against one of the waist-high pumpkins. "Really?"

She eyed me sharply. "I don't hold out much hope of it, mind you. The way your curses have been going, I expect he'll be prince of the Uplands first."

"Oh, Grandmother, thank you. I'll do it. I will. I—"

"Enough!" she snapped. "I don't need maudlin gratitude. You've still got a lot to learn, Prunella. Being a Bogthistle isn't just about having warts or turning someone into a frog. But I can't teach you that. You'll have to figure it out yourself. Out there." She jabbed one finger to the north. I did not move.

"Off with you now," she said. "Go on."

"G-go?" I stammered. "You're throwing me out?"

She didn't say anything more. Instead, she pursed her lips, whistling an eerie wavering call like the wail of a ghost. From somewhere out in the darkness came a low grumbling bellow.

"You're setting Yeg on me?" My feet were lead, my thoughts a flock of crows, wheeling and turning in madcap flight. She couldn't do this. It could not be happening.

Grandmother spun on her heel and stalked into the alchemy shop. The door slammed. I was never, ever, going to get inside. The closed door stared back at me. My future. Gone.

The bellow sounded again, closer. I shook myself. I still had one hope. I just needed to curse Barnaby. And for that, we both needed to be alive. Besides, a bog-witch would not give up. She would find a way to make things work. I drew in a steadying breath.

I grabbed the boy's elbow, pointing toward the mass of cypress trees that bounded the bottom of the garden. "This way." We ran, Yeg's thunderous bellows ringing through the night behind us.

Chapter 2

I leapt over a soggy pool, then bounded onward, past the bent cypress knees that poked up from the mire. Barnaby cursed as his slick boots skidded across a fallen log, nearly sending him flying. The ground shook with Yeg's pursuit. Trees cracked, splintered, and fell behind us.

As I ran, I searched the swamp for anything useful. The trinkets and herbs tied to my scarf clattered and chimed, but none of them could help me now. Nothing but the strongest of magics would stop Yeg. Magics I did not have.

I stomped down my fears. I would not waste this chance. I would prove Grandmother wrong. I might not be able to blast Yeg with a curse of fireballs, but I was still a Bogthistle. I would make do with what I had: my wits, my charms, and Barnaby the thief-hero.

We raced onward. The ground turned firmer, broken

by jutting granite boulders. The crash of falling trees and an endless chilling scrape of scaly skin pursued us. Barnaby had produced a short but wicked-looking dagger somewhere along the way. It wouldn't do much against Yeg, but it was something.

Finally, we staggered into a clearing, both of us panting for breath. The slithering seemed to come from all sides, as if some vast serpent had coiled around us. I looked to the moon, hoping to find some reassurance in that watchful silver eye. All I could see was a gossamer shimmer, like a fine fog, clinging to the trees. Vast webs veiled the treetops, turning the moonlight into a distant glow. Wonderful. If Yeg didn't eat us, the giant spiders would.

"Blast it!" Barnaby gestured ahead. More luminous webbing clouded our route. "We can't go this way. We'll get stuck in the webs, and I've been trussed up enough for one night, thank you very much." He spun around, searching the dark woods.

"That's it!" I started forward.

"Are you crazy?" Barnaby jerked my elbow. "Do you *want* to get eaten by a giant spider?"

I shook him off. "If we can make it through, Yeg won't be able to follow. Swamp-spider webs are as strong as ironwood. That ought to slow him down, at least enough for us to get away. It's a better chance than just running."

Barnaby looked dubious.

"You got into my grandmother's garden," I said. "Don't you think you can squirm past a few webs?"

Barnaby sniffed indignantly. "Of course *I* can. I was thinking of you. You're not exactly dressed for it, in that pile of rags. You won't get three feet without catching your hair. I reckon you'll end up a spider's midnight snack."

"You don't need to worry about me," I snapped. "I can take care of myself." I pulled the shawl from my shoulders and knotted it around my waist, out of the way. Pile of rags indeed! I wadded my cloud of loose black hair at the nape of my neck and tied it with two of the smaller braided bits.

Barnaby shrugged. "All right. Let's go."

I led the way into the spider grove, ducking under gauzy curtains, stepping carefully over the unidentifiable withered lumps that dangled from silken strands. A bellow sounded, closer than ever. Bits of leaf and fragments of web floated down to catch in my hands and tangle in my hair. My heart thudded in my throat.

Barnaby gave a low whistle as he glanced back. "Filthy fens! Will you look at the size of that thing?

That's the biggest gator I've ever seen!" He crowded behind me. "Hurry up!"

"I'm going as fast as I can." I tried to focus on the maze of clinging threads.

"Not fast enough!" Barnaby seized my arm, pulling me sideways, down a narrow web-spun corridor. I risked a look behind us, then wished I hadn't.

Gleaming green eyes advanced from the darkness. Rows of pale teeth yawned open, while the bulk of his massive trunklike body remained lost in the gloom. Strands of spidersilk clung to Yeg here and there, not nearly enough to stop him. He stalked closer. I pulled free from Barnaby's grip.

"Are you crazy?" he called. "What are you doing?"

"Slowing him down. You might want to hold on to something." I drew in my breath, concentrating on the air held tight in my lungs, willing it to do as I wished. It was a simple spell. Aunt Flywell used it to whisk the best of the bacon right off the platter, beating the rest of us every morning. If I could get it right, it just might save us.

I let out a piercing if slightly off-key whistle.

"Don't be stupid!" Barnaby said. "What if you—"

The rest of his warning was lost as a gust of air smashed into me, knocking me off my feet. Currents tore at my hair. Sticky threads filled the air. I flailed, reaching for something to steady me, but found nothing. Somewhere, Yeg bellowed.

The wind died down abruptly. I could just make out the massive, ridge-backed form of Yeg, enveloped in webs.

For a moment, my spirits rose. I would have jumped up and down in delight. But I couldn't jump. In fact, I couldn't move at all. I dangled in midair, trussed up tight in a cocoon of spidersilk.

"Bellow all you want, you big scaly lump, but the bog-witch wins this one," Barnaby called out as he clambered to his feet below me. "I take it back, Prunella; that spell was spiffing amazing!" He stopped, realizing I was not beside him any longer. "Prunella?"

"Up here," I growled. "And if you so much as chuckle, I swear—"

Barnaby stared up at me and gave a whoop of laughter.

It was unbearable. I tried to kick myself free.

He stopped laughing. "No, wait! You'll just get"— Barnaby groaned—"stuck even worse."

My attempts to free myself had set me whirling like a spindle, gathering even more threads. I bit down on my own bellow of frustration. Taking a long, steadying breath, I said, "All right, you slithery sneak-thief. Get me out of this."

If I had thought Barnaby's grin simply irritating back in Grandmother's garden, I was wrong. It was infuriating. He raised his brows, tapping the blade of his dagger against his arm. "Hmm . . . I suppose I am on a heroic quest. I ought to rescue the maiden in peril."

"Shut up and cut me free, you idiot."

"Even if she has the sharpest tongue in the lands." He made no move to cut me down. "Tell me, witch girl, why should I help you? You've already ruined my best jacket. I think I'm safer with you bundled up here in the bog, where you can't curse anyone else."

"You're just like all the stupid Uplanders," I said. I turned my head, staring into the shadowy treetops. Had something just moved? I tried to ignore it. "You think we're a bunch of evil hags."

"Oh, you mean you're not going to try to turn me into a frog?"

I gritted my teeth.

"On the other hand, I reckon that oil-dousing you gave me is the only reason I'm not caught, too."

"Just go on if you're going to leave me," I snapped. "I'd rather not listen to you babble."

"Tell you what," he said. "I'll cut you loose if you promise not to turn me into a frog."

My angry response turned to a gasp. Something *was*

moving up above me. Something with glittering eyes and too many legs.

"Fine, yes, I won't turn you into a frog. Now, get me out of here," my voice rose squeakily.

Three quick slices of Barnaby's dagger sent me thumping ungracefully to the ground. I didn't even bother to brush the leaves and moss from my backside. "We need to get somewhere safe before Yeg breaks free," I said. "And before something else tries to eat us."

Barnaby followed my wary glance toward the tree-tops and nodded. "You're the bog-witch. D'you have someplace in mind?"

Barnaby didn't think much of spending the night on a pile of leaves, but the hollow in the heights of the iron-wood tree really was the safest place I could think of. It was far enough from the fens to be spider-free, and even Yeg couldn't crunch through ironwood. The lofty hollow was warm, sheltered, even cozy. Besides, I was tired enough that I could have slept on the back of a galloping spectral stallion.

Waking was more difficult. I kept my eyes tightly closed, indulging in the pretense that I was still back in my snug chamber at home. But instead of Ezzie's snores, I heard the warbling of vireos and the hum of needlewings. I smelled the fragrance of wild hot-leaf blooms, not the scent of smoky bacon and sizzling griddlecakes. There were no chattering aunts downstairs to tell me terrifying, exhilarating stories of their adventures while we sorted herbs and wove marsh-grass charm dollies. A pit opened inside me as every happy memory slipped from my grasp, falling down, down, down into darkness. How could I bear this? My family were all I knew. And now they had thrown me out, like dirty wash-water.

I forced my eyes open. I'd luxuriated in misery long enough. It was time to get to work. I stood, shaking the leaves from my skirt. An alarming number of them wouldn't budge, stuck to the bits of spiderweb that clung to me still. Well, I supposed it contributed to my witchly appearance. Even if I didn't have warts.

I wrinkled my nose, seeing Barnaby still asleep on the other side of the hollow. He lay with one arm across his face, the other flung over his weathered pack. Even in sleep, his fingers gripped the leather straps tightly. Now that the sun was out and we no longer had a giant alligator trying to eat us, I had the opportunity to study the boy more closely.

He was the lanky type, but without any unfortunate gawkiness, unless you counted his shaggy hair. Rather well dressed, too. Even a bit foppish, with that gold braid edging his oil-stained jacket and a froth of lace on his shirt collar. I sniffed. My own dress might be dingy, and my scarf might be tattered, but they were comfortable and serviceable, and that was what mattered to me.

I flexed my fingers. It seemed somehow unsporting, when he was lying there so peacefully. He had cut me loose from the webs, after all. And no one had ever complimented my spells before. The best I'd gotten from Grandmother was a stiff nod. Barnaby had called my wind spell "spiffing amazing." Even now the memory made me grin.

I forced a scowl back onto my face. I didn't need compliments from an Uplander. I could not leave the bog. I would never survive out there. What would I do if a mob of angry Uplanders set on me with torches? Shower them with more alligator spoor?

I took a deep breath, then raised my crooked finger. I wasn't really breaking my word. It was his own fault he hadn't phrased the promise better. I muttered the incantation.

Nothing happened. I began again, a little more loudly. I was halfway through when Barnaby rolled over. He scrabbled back from me, blinking in the murky light that filtered through the vine-tangled opening. "What d'you think you're doing?"

"Did you feel something? Did it start to work?" Hope billowed my spirits. I could be back home by teatime.

"No!" Barnaby leapt from the pile of leaves.

"It must have been working. You're running away!"

"I'm running away because it's blasted annoying. You promised you'd stop."

"I wasn't trying to turn you into a *frog*." I sniffed. "A toad is an entirely different creature."

He gave a huff. "I should have known not to trust the word of a bog-witch." He bent to retrieve his oily boots.

"I do keep my word," I said, brushing aside the pinpricks of guilt. "You ought to have listened more carefully. Oh, don't run off. I'll turn you back again right away. I just need to prove I can do it."

"You're insane," said Barnaby. He knocked his boots together, scattering clods of dark-brown mud. "The sooner I'm out of this crazy bog the better. Your granny was bad enough. Putting a death ward on a patch of asparagus? Sweet hills! And setting a giant alligator on her own granddaughter?" He shook his head. "But the craziest thing is that you want to be one of them. I mean, look at you. You could pass for a normal Uplander girl if you cleaned up and put on decent clothes. And you're nice enough under all those prickles; you saved my life back there. Now you're trying to turn me into a toad. Crazy," he said again, shoving a foot into one boot.

"I'd sooner toss myself into the pits than be some farm girl with ribbons in my hair and nothing in my head but the price of eggs and who I'm going to marry," I said. "I'm going to be the greatest bog-witch since Esmeralda herself. Then I *will* turn you into a frog. And I might not turn you back!"

"Come off it, Prunella," he said. "Even your own granny doesn't think you can do it."

Tears burned in my eyes. I blinked furiously. I would not let him see. "I know m-more than a s-stupid Uplander." Blast it all, my voice was crumbling like a biscuit in hot tea. I turned away, gulping down great breaths of steamy morning air.

After what felt like forever, Barnaby said, "Oh, filthy fens, Prunella. I didn't mean to— These Bottom-lands have me all inside out. I just want to get back home."

Me, too, I thought.

"Listen, I'm still not going to let you turn me into a frog, or a toad," he said. "But you've got more brass than I do. Bog-witch or not, you saved my life twice now. I reckon your old granny will show up soon enough, begging you to come back."

I doubted it. "I don't need you to feel sorry for me." I plunked myself down on the edge of the hollow to stare at the woods beyond. Coils of morning mist wove through the dense greenery.

"Fine. I won't." Barnaby sat down beside me, pulling on his other boot. "But I think it's crazy to *want* to be a bog-witch. You should hear the stories folks tell about you lot."

"I couldn't give a barrel of fish bait what a bunch of stupid Uplanders think. I just want my grand-mother to . . ."

"To what?"

Love me, I thought. Smile at me. It sounded pathetic. "To respect me," I said, finally. I leaned out, studying the blooming vines shielding our hiding spot. "Anyway, why do you care?" I plucked one of the large orange flowers. "Shouldn't you be hightailing it back to the Uplands?"

"I'd rather be kicking back on the veranda at the Peacock's Rest, that's for sure," Barnaby admitted. "But, like I said, you're not bad for a bog-witch. I've never seen anything like that wind spell. If you ask me, that's loads better than turning someone into a frog."

Something in my insides untwisted. I twirled the flower between my fingers, peeling back the leathery red-speckled petals, uncertain how to respond. It was just words, but I felt he'd given me a gift. "You're not bad for an Uplander, either," I said finally, handing him the bloom.

He stared at it.

"Haven't you ever drunk hot-leaf nectar?" I seized another for myself.

Barnaby looked oddly relieved. "Oh. Right. We just drink the tea in the Uplands. I thought . . . Never mind." He quickly raised the bloom to his mouth, then sneezed.

"Watch the pollen," I said, in between slurps of my own bloom. "What about you?" I asked. "Is recovering lost magical chalices your family trade?"

"Not exactly," he muttered. "I reckon my family's as mixed up as yours."

"Oh? How?"

Barnaby busied himself cleaning nonexistent mud from his cuffs. "Speaking of hightailing it back to the Uplands, I ought to get going. Drinking out of a flower isn't bad, but I still prefer the tea." He seized one of the thick hot-leaf vines and began lowering himself down from the tree.

"Going." The word clanged inside me, turning my insides empty. I ought to be happy. If I couldn't curse him, what use was he? Yes, he'd said a few nice things. But he was also overdressed, overconfident, and too blasted charming for his own good. What did I need with a thief-hero like Barnaby?

I gasped as an idea bubbled up in my mind. That was it! I knew exactly how to prove myself to Grandmother. I could already see myself marching back, triumphant, our greatest treasure in my hands. Aunt Flywell would bake pumpkin cakes, and they'd make a bonfire and hang the banners just like we did when anyone came home after a long trip. Oh, Ezzie would be so jealous!

Brimming with new determination, I thumped down to the mossy ground a moment later. I found Barnaby turning a slow circle, eyeing the thick woods on all sides. "D'you think you could set me off in the right direction?"

"We should go this way." I set off along the narrow path I'd indicated, only to pause a few steps later. "Well? Aren't you coming? I thought you were all afire to get back to your precious Uplands."

He looked at me with an intensity that made blood rush to my cheeks. "What?" I demanded. "Have I got mud on my nose or something?"

"No . . . it's just . . . you want to come along?"

"Where else am I going to go?"

"And you mean to just walk into the Uplands looking like that?"

"Like what?"

He waved his fingers around his own face and hair. "You know, all hag-from-the-bog."

"I am a hag from the bog." I raised a hand to pat my braids. I kept a lot of things tied to my braids, and to the fringes of my scarf. It seemed more sensible than carrying around a hulking big pack. If I needed a bit of loon feather or a silver spoon for a charm, there it was, right in reach, and no need to worry about losing it or forgetting it. Besides, it helped to counteract my snub-nosed, wartless features. I should be happy, I told myself. Clearly it was working.

Barnaby grimaced. "You've got a dried chicken foot in your hair."

"I need that to keep away the— Oh, I don't have to explain it to you." I wasn't about to tell Barnaby I was terrified of pondswaggles. "All got up like a fancy-dandy prince when you're really just a sneak-thief who likes to pillage bog-witch alchemy shops. And *your* hair looks like you cut it all off with a butter knife, so you needn't make fun of mine."

Barnaby, who was normally pale as milk, couldn't hide his angry flushes. "I'm not a thief! I'm on a quest for the Mirable Chalice. And I don't need you tagging along, making me look ridiculous. I'll find my own way back home. It's not as if we're traveling together."

Barnaby marched away angrily. I had to stop him. He was my only chance to regain my home, my family.

"I know where the Mirable Chalice is," I called out.

He stopped. He stared back at me with such a strange expression. Fear? Hope?

"You can't," he said, finally, with a slight tremble in his voice.

I drew on every ounce of witchliness I could muster. "It's in the treasure house of Lord Blackthorn, wizard of the Mistveil Bayou. My grandmother herself said it was there." She hadn't said exactly that, but where else would it be?

Barnaby's shoulders sagged. Why did he look so relieved? Perhaps I just didn't understand how to read the faces of boys.

"It's sure to be well protected, but if you managed to get into Grandmother's garden you ought to be able to get past Blackthorn's traps and wards. Especially if you have me along to help."

He still hadn't said anything. "It's the only place that makes sense," I said. "Blackthorn tried to steal the chalice once already."

Barnaby licked his lips. "Lord Blackthorn, you say?" He rubbed a hand over his thatch of hair. It did not improve the shaggy mess. "But that was two hundred years ago. Shouldn't he be dead?"

"He's still alive. Or, at least, he's not dead." I told him about Grandmother's nightly curses and the stolen grimoire.

"So he's just been holed up in his bayou all this time with your great-great-granny's magic book? Just sitting around stewing over being kicked out of the Uplands and not getting to raise the hosts of frights from the bog and doom everyone?"

"Something like that."

"You're saying he dragged his raggedy, two-hundred-year-old bones into the Uplands and just grabbed the chalice? Or do you reckon he sent his jacks?" Barnaby snorted. "And no one happened to notice a pack of spindly, pumpkin-headed scarecrows with flaming eyes marching around the countryside?"

"I don't know," I said, waving away the details. "Maybe he spent two hundred years figuring out how to do it properly. Who else would have stolen it?"

"Lord Blackthorn. Hmm. Yeah. That makes sense," said Barnaby. Something flickered across his features. I knew that expression well enough, for I'd felt it on my own face: a thinking look, a crafty look. "And why would you do all this? A bog-witch trying to save the Uplands from the curse?"

"I couldn't care less for your stinking Uplands and your inns and fancy clothes." I crossed my arms. "What

I do care about is Esmeralda's grimoire. If anything can teach me how to be a proper bog-witch, it's that book. Once I've got it, Grandmother will have to let me come back." I tilted my head, fingering the loon feather on the tip of one braid. "Is the curse very bad?"

He scuffed at the dirt. "A little corn gone bad and a few sniffles and people call it a curse. If folks knew what it was really like when your belly aches from hunger and you haven't got—" He stopped short, then shrugged. "Anyway, it's not the first time anyone's been dealt a rotten hand."

"That's hardly a heroic thing to say."

He smirked. "Tell me I'm not a hero when girls are throwing flowers at my feet and all the Uplands are cheering for Barnaby the Brave."

"That's why you're doing this? For the fame?"

Barnaby gave me an affronted look. "What do you take me for?" He grinned. "There's fortune, too, of course. The queen's offering a mighty fine reward." He straightened his gilt-edged jacket. "I'm not heartless, though. I'll make sure the sniffles and corn rot get taken care of."

I shrugged. "So—do we have a deal?"

He hefted his pack, cocking his head to look me up and down once more. "Can you at least get rid of the chicken foot?"

I untied the withered thing from my braid. How likely was it that I'd run into a pondswaggle in the Uplands? Just in case, I secured it to a bit of the fringe on the underside of my shawl, out of sight. Then I stuck out my hand.

"Deal," he said, smiling as he shook my hand. Hope throbbed in me like the call of a bullfrog over the empty bog. Once I got Barnaby to Blackthorn Manor, he'd do my work for me. Then I'd have Esmeralda's grimoire, and Grandmother would take me back.

I just needed to survive long enough in the Uplands to get there.

Chapter 3

I stood on the threshold of the Uplands, my heart hammering so loud I was sure Barnaby must hear it. Ahead, the trail proceeded from the fringe of cattails, winding up into green hills toward the peaked roofs and towers of Withywatch. I squinted, searching for any sparkle of magic ahead. All I could see were neat fences and placid cows chewing their cud. It was horrible.

Behind me, the bog throbbed with life and magic. One more step forward. That was all it would take. I ran my hands over the shells and feathers and herbs knotted to my shawl. There, at least, I caught the half-seen sparkle of the magic that had seeped into the trinkets.

I'd been collecting components all morning. It wasn't much: a tiny cupful to sustain me through the magicless desert of the Uplands. I could fill a room with flame and smoke, summon several good downpours of alligator spoor, that sort of thing. But that was all. And when it was gone . . .

No, I told myself. I would be back long before then. And with Esmeralda's grimoire in hand. There would be a bonfire, and we'd have stuffed pumpkins, and cursing contests, and I'd win them all. Until then, I'd just have to leave behind the fluting of the frogs and the strong, living, green scent of the bog. I looked out over the flame grasses as they tossed their ruddy heads in the morning sun. I snapped off a stalk and wove it into one of my braids, something to remind me of home. Also very useful in protective charms and finding spells. I considered gathering an entire armful, but it would be cumbersome to carry.

Barnaby gave an enormous sigh. He stretched out his arms, grinning as he looked ahead to the town. "I can't wait to get to a proper inn again." He rolled his shoulders to settle the straps of his pack. "A real bed. Sausages and cheese. D'you know, I ate eel for three days straight out there in that bog? And some *nasty* red berries. I couldn't unpucker for half a day, those things were so sour."

"Cranberries are perfectly delicious with enough honey," I retorted. "The Bottomlands aren't *that* bad."

He snorted. "It'll take a lot of honey to sweeten me on anything from the Bottomlands. Alligators. Deadly asparagus. Bog-witches." He realized I was glaring at him. "What? I didn't mean you. You're different."

That was the problem. I stifled my sigh and stepped forward. It was time to face the Uplands. Lord Blackthorn's demesne in the Mistveil Bayou was a part of the Bottomlands, but it lay on the other side of the Sangue River Bay, too wide to cross directly. We would have to travel through the northern hills for several weeks to reach it.

How many times had Grandmother warned me against leaving the bog? The Bottomlands were our home. They were safe, a place where magic still flowed in a shivery glimmering mist all around, if you slitted your eyes and looked crossways at it.

The Uplands were strange. They were full of people who chucked stones and brandished pitchforks, full of orderly green fields and pale highways and not a speck of magic, except what had been imprisoned in artifacts and enchantments long ago.

The trail turned to hard-packed earth as we progressed farther into the hills. My feet missed the spongy softness of moss and mud. We joined a wider road, passing between fields of knee-high corn toward the city wall. We drew even with a youth leading a donkey. His stare was sharp enough to bore holes in my skin.

I gulped against the tightness that had suddenly seized my throat.

The boy reached for something on his belt that glinted in the sun. I tensed, remembering hateful words and the tines of pitchforks against the sky. Then I saw what he grasped in his spindly fingers: a wrought-silver circle.

"That's for warding off wraiths, donkey boy," I snapped, unable to hold down the jittery feeling any longer. "And if you keep staring like that, the crows are going to come along and pluck your eyes clean out of your empty head."

"Prunella!" Barnaby hustled me along the road double-time until the boy had vanished behind the next hill. "Could you possibly try not to insult everyone we meet?"

"Me?" I tugged my arm free. "*He* was the one staring at me like I was a gobbet of mudwhelp slime. And did you see that talisman? I'm no wraith!"

Barnaby let out an exasperated breath. "You're the one who wants to walk around looking like the spawn of the pits. You can't blame him."

"I'm not putting on petticoats and a frilly cap just so some brainless donkey boy doesn't have a fit."

Barnaby rolled his eyes. "Wonderful. We aren't even

inside the city gates and I'm regretting this. I think I'd be better off finding Blackthorn on my own."

"No," I said hastily. "I can do this." I untied my shawl from where I'd knotted it around my waist, then wrapped it around my head and shoulders. "See? That's better, isn't it?"

Barnaby looked me over dubiously. "Maybe if you don't speak. I suppose the Tipsy Coon won't be particular as long as we've got coins to buy our room and board."

"We're *staying* here?" I tried to keep the tremor out of my voice. Bad enough I had to go into the city for an hour, let alone sleep there.

"I'm not going anywhere until I've cleaned up and had a decent meal," Barnaby said. "You can stay out here and find another pile of leaves to sleep in; I'll look you up in a few days, after I've got the taste of eel off my tongue."

As unpleasant as it was being in the Uplands with Barnaby, it would be ten times worse to be alone there. What if that donkey boy came after me with a pitchfork? I'd seen the sparkle in his eye, like the reflection of torches about to light a bonfire.

"No! I mean, I've got to keep an eye on you."

Barnaby arched a brow. "I didn't think you cared."

"I don't," I retorted. "I need you to help me get that

grimoire. And you need me to get that chalice." I gathered up my courage. "I've walked across the flaming mire. I ought to be able to survive in an Uplander city for one night."

"Two," said Barnaby. "Maybe three if the tailor's busy. Hey, now, no grumbling. I have to look good, to balance you out. Come on, I know one thing that'll make you want to stay awhile. You ever have fried bread?"

"See? I told you," said Barnaby, looking far too smug for his own good.

"It's . . . not bad," I said, trying desperately not to stuff the entire wedge of fried dough into my mouth at once. The thief-hero was right. It was the best thing I'd ever eaten: light and crispy and speckled with cinnamon and nutmeg. I swallowed my last generous bite. "It'd be better with cranberry jam," I said, struggling valiantly not to look back at the bread-seller's cart.

"Oh? Not bad?" He tossed the last bit of his own cake into the air, catching it adroitly in his open mouth. "So you don't want another, then?"

I bit my lip. He laughed. "Wait here."

I watched him jog back the way we'd come. So far, so good. No one had tried to put me on a bonfire yet. I had gotten plenty of strange looks, however. Even now, an old man at the tea shop across the street was staring at me through his pipe smoke. I pulled my scarf more closely around my face and checked that the chicken foot wasn't showing. Two of the barmaids giggled and pointed. My heart pounding, insults fighting to leap out of my mouth, I pretended to study the shop on the other side of the street.

It didn't require much pretense, for this was a marvelous shop. Leather-bound spines marched along the shelves on display behind the wide front window. I pressed my nose to the glass, squinting at the titles eagerly. The Bogthistle library was extensive, but consisted entirely of spell-books, cookbooks, swamp menageries, and a handful of Aunt Flywell's saucy novels, which Ezzie and I weren't allowed to read but sneaked out anyway. I studied the display, hoping to find something new and interesting, perhaps an account of the exotic Palm Isles, or a book of ghost stories. The first few titles were not promising: *Ten Rules of Successful Animal Husbandry* and *Lady Ainsley's Guide to Popular Fashion* and that sort of thing.

The titles on the second shelf were more encouraging, and included a book on unusual gems and minerals, a treatise on growing mushrooms, and a number of other intriguing volumes. I squinted, catching a stray glimmer. No, I wasn't imagining things. Some of these books were magical! *Wards Against the Bog-Spawn* had only the faintest glint, but *Mother Elda's Book of Practical Herbcraft* had sparks dancing along the spine. They must be very old, enchanted by some sorcerer back in Esmeralda's day.

Something was odd, though. The glimmer of magic seemed to be shifting, rising off the books like mist over a pool in the morning sun. I was tilting my head, trying to get a better look, when I saw something that drove all these thoughts from my mind: a thin black tome with dim silver lettering that read *Secrets of the Mistveil*.

I whirled around, looking for Barnaby. This book could mean the difference between walking out of the Mistveil Bayou alive and ending up in a mirethane's stewpot. We had to have it.

There he was, lounging against the side of the bread-seller's cart, talking to a girl. Not a milkmaid in a frilly cap, either: This young woman was fine stuff, and she knew it. She held her lacy fan above her lips, promising secrets. Barnaby said something I couldn't make out, and the girl ducked her head, smiling. He held out one of the two cakes in his hand. The girl took the fried bread—my fried bread!—with a smile, and began nibbling one edge daintily.

Fine. If he'd rather waste time on some simpering

bundle of lace and ribbons, I'd just go get the book myself. I stomped into the shop, rather more wrathfully than I intended. The door swung shut with a bang. A man with the pale, reedy look of a parsnip stood behind the counter. He skittered to one side as I approached, so that the heavy wooden slab stood between us.

"I want to see that book in the window," I said. "*Secrets of the Mistveil.*"

"Excuse me?"

I pushed back the muffling scarf to repeat myself. Parsnip man gave a shiver, his lip curling. "I'm afraid that's rather expensive," he said. "And quite old."

"If it's worth it, we'll pay," I said. I could try my seeming spell to turn leaves into coins. Or, if that flopped, Barnaby could pay up and live without a spare jacket.

"I can't allow my most valuable wares to be handled by . . ." He gulped under my narrowed gaze, but went on. "Things are bad enough with the curse. Half my best tomes are fading. I won't have them getting mud-stained and stinking of the bog." He looked down to my hands, gripping the edge of the counter.

Dirt was crusted under my nails. I jerked them to my sides. "I want to see that book," I said.

Parsnip man looked past me, out to the street. Stinking sloughs, he was going to make a scene. He'd start caterwauling that there was a loathsome bog-witch in his shop. I'd be up on a bonfire before I knew it, and Barnaby wouldn't even notice, too busy chatting up fan girl. My stomach turned over; my skin shivered with the thought of fire.

I fumbled through my hair for the coin-shaped leaves of wild ginger, then seized the tiny lump of fool's gold from its pouch on my scarf. It felt oddly sticky, but there was no time to clean it off. This fellow deserved to be cheated. I stood ready, my heart pounding.

"Go on, then, get along," the shopkeeper said, licking his lips.

"I'm not leaving without that book," I insisted. "And you can't say no to this."

I brought my hands together, intoning the seeming spell as I did.

Instead of a shower of gold coins, a blazing green fire whooshed up. My heart galloped off into some distant land, leaving me staring foolishly at the inferno.

Smoke roiled as the verdant flames raced along the counter, devouring a few scrolls and curling up a stack of small notebooks. Parsnip man scrambled back, throwing his arms out to shield the stacks of books behind him. His wide, desperate eyes found me, reflecting fire and fear. "It's yours!" he cried. "Take it! Here!" He darted for the shelf in the window, sending books crashing to the floor as he pulled free *Secrets of the Mistveil*. "Just stop it! Don't burn my store down!"

He thrust it toward me. I reached out, my mind spinning. What had I done? I stared at the black tome in my hand, then yelped as flames burst around the leather bindings with a sudden crackle. It was on fire!

And so was *I*! I dropped the burning book to slap at my arms. I felt no pain, but green flames danced across my eyes. Was this what Grandmother's flaming-eye charm was like?

My heart pounded so loud it sounded like running footsteps. No, there *were* footsteps. Someone was behind me. Hands gripped my shoulders. I had one last horrified look at the shopkeeper before I was hurled out the door, into the street. Someone propelled me along. I scrabbled at the air, trying to clear my vision.

"Hold on," said Barnaby. "I just need to find— Ah, that'll do."

The hands on my back pushed me down, and suddenly I was soaking wet. Cold water flooded my nose. The green flames winked out. I pushed myself back up. Rivulets streamed down my face. I was soaked through. "A rain barrel?" I sputtered.

"Stay here," said Barnaby. He shoved his pack into my hands, stripped off his jacket, and dredged it through the water. "Let me play my part now." He nodded at the pack. "Just keep that safe, will you?" Then he winked and ran off, back around the corner.

I twisted the heavy sack between my fingers, which were still sticky, and blinked through dripping eyelashes at the narrow street around me. I saw no one besides me and the rain barrel. But I could hear shouts, and I could smell smoke. A piteous wail curdled the air.

I couldn't bear this. It might not be very witchlike, but I wasn't just going to stand there and let all those beautiful papers go up in smoke. Though I couldn't curse, I could do something. If nothing else, I could smother the flames with my own soggy self.

I brushed my sopping hair back over my shoulders and started off. But as I reached the corner, the shop-keeper's wailing stopped. My footsteps slowed. Did that mean . . . ? Was he . . . ?

Don't be an idiot, I told myself firmly. It wasn't that big a fire. He had plenty of time to get out. Unless he was trying to save his books. I hesitated. Visions of what I might see swirled through my mind. Destruction. Death. All my fault.

I took a deep breath. I had to find out what I'd done. I peered around the corner cautiously.

A crowd of figures stood in the street, chattering and clamoring. The girl with the fan, the smoking gee-zer from the tea shop, the giggling girls, and more. At the center stood the shopkeeper, ash-stained but grinning broadly, and Barnaby. He stood in his simple white shirtsleeves, wearing a look of abashed humility.

". . . saved my entire shop," the bookseller was saying. "That bog-witch set it all afire, but this young man came to my rescue. Charged in without a care for himself and struck the flames out with his jacket. Saved it all. Even me!" The man held out his arms, turning to display the scorch marks across his own coat. The onlookers oohed and aahed.

"I can't thank you enough, lad," the shopkeeper went on. "How can I ever repay you?"

"Oh, it was nothing. A jacket is a small price to pay for saving a man's livelihood." Barnaby ducked his head, the picture of modesty.

"Piffle! I'll see you rewarded for your kindness, lad. There. That ought to buy you the finest jacket in town."

I watched, speechless. Even from here I could see the glint of the gold coins being pressed into Barnaby's hands.

"Oh, really, I couldn't . . ."

He did, though. Barnaby might protest, but he slipped the coins away quick as a wink. So quickly, in fact, that I hadn't quite seen where they'd ended up.

"Isn't there anything else I can do for you?"

"Well . . . if it's no trouble . . ."

"Anything!"

"I thought I might like that book, the one that the bog-witch wanted. Someone ought to find out what the despicable hag is after. Who knows what she might do next?"

A chorus of approving murmurs rose from the crowd. I balled up my fists and gritted my teeth. Oh, I'd show him what this bog-witch was going to do next.

I reminded myself that I needed Barnaby to get into Blackthorn's treasury. I couldn't afford to break his fingers or give him frostbite, and if I was going to be traveling with him I certainly wasn't going to try the skunk-stink curse or the doom of a hundred misfortunes.

I waited, listening to Barnaby accepting congratulations from what sounded like every citizen of Withywatch. At last he detached himself from the adoring masses. I heard him coming, whistling an irritatingly jaunty tune.

"Oof!" He gasped as the sack hit him in the midsection. "Hey!" He rubbed his chest, eyeing me reproachfully.

"It's not my fault you're carrying around lumps of iron," I said. "And, like you said, I'm a bog-witch. Who knows what I might do next?"

"You can't be angry at me. I just saved your backside from a merry roasting by the fine citizens of Withy-watch." He held out a charred oblong. "I hope this was worth it. Got pretty burnt by that fire of yours. Still, not a bad take. Generous fellow, that bookseller."

I stared at the book, then at him.

"Now, don't be like that. I couldn't have done it without you. And I was due for a new jacket in any case. I don't think I'd have ever gotten the bog stench out of the old one."

"You used me," I said, finally finding words. "You waltzed in and played the hero and let me look like a fool."

"Hey, now, you made a fool of yourself all on your own. And it wasn't as bad as you think. All right, so maybe it wasn't the swiftest choice in a room full of paper, but that flaming charm was frog-flipping spectacular."

I gargled something inarticulate. I still didn't understand what had gone wrong. I'd had the ginger, and the seeming spell should have created a shower of gold coins that would last a few days, then melt back into leaves. Now I'd wasted my fool's gold, which I'd traded off Ezzie at the cost of a dozen of my best crow feathers. I felt for the pouch where it hung from the fringe of my scarf. Then I frowned. It wasn't empty.

I pulled out a glimmering golden lump. "Stinking

sloughs!" I tightened my fist, remembering the sticky gob of pyre root I'd stuffed in there this morning. I had grabbed the wrong lump!

"Don't look so glum," Barnaby said. "Do you want another fried cake?"

What I wanted was to be able to do one thing properly. Fighting off bitterness, I tucked the fool's gold away again, making certain there was nothing else in the pouch this time.

Barnaby stretched his arms, yawning hugely. "Enough heroics. I'd give my left ear for a bath and lunch." He hitched the pack over one shoulder and set off down the street. "But first we're finding you some new clothes."

I grimaced.

"Unless you want to get run out of town by an angry mob . . . ?"

"Fine," I said. "These are pretty muddy. But no lace. And no ruffles. And I'm keeping my scarf."

I raised a disdainful brow at the blue dress Master Morland held up. "I said no lace."

"Come on, Prunella. It's not half bad," said Barnaby. "You'd look swell in it. No one would think you were a"—he glanced at the shopkeeper—"not from around here."

"Because I'd look like any other girl off the street. Besides, those sleeves are so puffed I'd be afraid to put it on. The first bit of wind might pouf me up into the sky."

Master Morland's hopeful smile faded. "But they've all got lace and puffed sleeves. My dear Mary made—makes—them all that way. It's the fashion."

"The fashion needs to change, then," I muttered. "Maybe I'd have better luck looking at the men's clothing."

Master Morland made a clucking sort of noise in the back of his throat, but led me over to a long rack of jackets and breeches.

I shook my head. "There's even more lace over here." And that wasn't the worst of it. Oh, they were beautifully made, stitched of fine rich fabric in shimmering jewel tones. But they were all the same. Like a garden with row upon row of beautiful, identical tulips. I wanted a spotted spider-trap orchid.

"Now, that's more like it," said Barnaby gleefully, hastening to one end of the rack. "Right spiff that is. I'll be as fine as a prince." He gathered up the armful of green velvet and dashed behind the changing screen.

I turned on Master Morland. "Isn't there anything else?"

His dark cheeks rounded out as he considered my question. "Well, there are a few things in the back wardrobe. But you wouldn't want those. No one wants those.

Just my dear Mary having a bit of fun. Waste of good cloth, I used to tell her, but it made her so happy, I—" The man choked off, rubbing one hand across his face. "Well, come along back, and you can see for yourself."

Master Morland led me to a tall mahogany armoire tilted up against the rear wall of the shop, between a pile of hatboxes and a curtained doorway. The heavy door creaked open at his touch to reveal a jumble of colors and shapes.

I clapped my hands together. "Perfect!"

"What's wrong with it?" I asked a short time later, as I spun around admiring my new skirt.

"There are so many answers to that question." Barnaby's eyebrows had been lodged up around his hairline since I walked out from behind the changing screen. "For one, it's green."

"So is your suit."

"Forest green. Not pea-soup green."

"It's purple, too."

"Exactly."

I ignored his look. "I think it's quite fetching. Even with these little orange flowers embroidered all along the bottom. They remind me of hot-leaf blossoms. And the skirt and jacket together are half the price of your breeches alone."

I liked the matching short coat even better than the

skirt. It had voluminous pockets and flared comfortably at the waist. I frowned, noticing that I'd already gotten a bit of pyre-root sap on one of the star-shaped ivory buttons. The cursed stuff was impossible to get off!

Barnaby sighed. "We'll take it all," he told Master Morland.

The shopkeeper smiled. "Oh, Mary would be—will be—so pleased. No one's ever bought anything from the back of the shop."

"Is she traveling?" Barnaby asked, glancing around the shop as he handed Master Morland several gold coins.

"Oh no. She's . . ." The shopkeeper fumbled with the coins as he locked them away in a money box. "I suppose everyone knows. That's why business has been so poor lately. It's the curse, you see."

Barnaby stiffened. Two sharp lines creased his forehead. "She's been cursed?"

"My poor girl. Used to be she had more gumption and spice than a cradle of kittens. Now she just lies there. Barely eats. Been a couple of others taken ill, too, all the same way. It's horrible." He shook his head. "I look after the shop best I can, keep an eye on her in the back." He jerked his chin toward the curtained door at the rear of the shop.

"Can we meet her?" Barnaby asked abruptly.

"I suppose it wouldn't hurt," said Master Morland. "I've had every apothecary and healer I could find in to have a look. Been about as helpful as wings on a pig."

Barnaby ignored my questioning glance and followed Master Morland. I tarried for a moment. It didn't seem like the wisest or safest choice, but my curiosity had been piqued, and I felt I owed the woman something. I really did love that star-buttoned jacket.

The chamber was tiny, half of it filled by the narrow cot where Mary Morland lay. I hung back. Something about the chilliness, the stillness of that thin figure sent fingers of fear rippling down my spine. Even from the doorway I could see the dark hollows under her eyes and the beads of sweat clinging to her half-opened lips.

Master Morland leaned over the bed, taking his wife's hand as if it were a bit of fine porcelain. "Mary, dear, these young people wanted to meet you. The young master's got up in one of your best suits. And look, this young lady's taken a liking to that green-and-purple fancy from the big wardrobe. You know, the one I always said looked like a collision between a bowl of pea soup and a—" He looked at me and cleared his throat. "Well, you know the one I mean."

Slowly, she blinked. Her gaze drifted, meandering down from the ceiling to Master Morland's nose, to

Barnaby's sleeve, to me. I swallowed, forcing myself to step forward.

Mary trembled, her breath catching. Her eyes met mine, and something sparked in the depths. Her hand spasmed, clutching the thin blue blanket covering her chest. My stomach buzzed with my wish to be gone, away from that still form and those restless, hungry eyes. I recoiled. She blinked again, and her eyes slipped back into dullness.

"How do you know it's a curse?" asked Barnaby, his fingers shaking slightly, though his voice was firm.

"Same as the rest. It started round the time word came about the Mirable Chalice."

Barnaby looked at me with an unfamiliar intensity. "What do you think? Is it a curse?"

I reached back for the doorframe, still shaken. I didn't want that hungry look latching on to me again. From the safety of the doorway, I squinted at Mary and gasped.

"What?" Barnaby demanded. "What is it?"

I slitted my eyes again, certain I must be imagining things. But no, there it was, a faint shimmer. Just like I'd seen over the books in the shop. The thin cloud shivered with each of Mary's exhalations, drifting slowly up and away. I turned, tracking the glints. But the trail was so weak I lost it before I'd gone two steps into the front of the shop.

I turned back to Barnaby and Master Morland, who had followed me out. "But it doesn't make sense. Why would she have magic? And why would it be wasting away? Where is it going?"

"Magic? My Mary?" Master Morland waved his hand across his eyes in the warding against evil. "She might make a few odd bits of clothing here and there, but that's not magic. She's no stinking witch from the fens."

"I'm sure that's not what Prunella means," said Barnaby soothingly. "Everyone knows Uplanders don't do magic. It's just the curse, right? You can see that there's an evil magic on poor Mary?"

I hesitated. That did make more sense. But if the curse magic was drifting away, why wasn't Mary getting better? I shook my head. "I don't know . . . It's hard to tell. Everything's so different here."

Master Morland appeared only slightly mollified. Barnaby whisked me out of the shop on a tide of praise for Mary's work and wishes for her quick recovery.

We walked on in silence. Mary Morland's eyes haunted my thoughts. What was going on? Was it a curse?

"You'd better be careful what you say," Barnaby grumbled. "It's not as if that outfit's going to blend into the cobblestones."

"Whereas no one will notice you at all," I said dryly.

"It's good to be noticed if it's in the right way," Barnaby said, stretching out his arms so that the green velvet and gold braid shone in the afternoon sun. He tipped his feathered cap to a passing girl, who smiled back over her basket of freshly washed linens.

"So where's this Drunken Possum of yours?" I asked. Whatever was going on with this supposed curse, we wouldn't find answers here. I quickened my steps.

"It's called the Tipsy Coon."

"Whatever. Just as long as the food's as good as you say it is."

We entered the swinging half-door beneath a placard depicting a dancing raccoon balancing a potbellied jug on its head. Inside, Barnaby chose a table set into an alcove near the hearth. A man wearing a stained leather apron and gold rings in his ears took our order of sausage and rice and molasses pie. There was a full pot of hot-leaf tea to wash it down. Barnaby took his with milk, but I liked it better straight, so that my nose tingled with each spicy sip.

As we ate, I studied the tavern. It didn't look like much: dark, smoky, and peopled with sour-faced men and women who might have given even Grandmother a turn.

"The food's tasty, I'll give you that," I told Barnaby,

around mouthfuls of pepper-flecked sausage. "But isn't this place a little rustic for you?"

"If you go back and get the blue dress and take all that clutter out of your hair, we can stay at the Peacock's Rest," he offered. "They've got a palm garden and porcelain teapots."

I snorted. "I don't need frills and fripperies. I just need a good night's sleep. We've got a long way to go."

"Right." Barnaby jerked his thumb at the map spread out on the table between us. "It's a long trek from the soot stain to the charred hole."

I suppressed my sigh. *Secrets of the Mistveil* hadn't fared well in the fire. I'd puzzled out a few intriguing but maddeningly unclear phrases:

> *. . . no doom, but a ruse to gain . . .*
> *. . . saw his mistake and tried to recover the . . .*
> *. . . lands stripped of their magic to serve her . . .*
> *. . . retreated to the lowlands where yet remained . . .*
> *. . . knowledge to break the curse of the chalice . . .*

The only really useful thing that had survived was a map in the center. Unfortunately, half the map was now charred, riddled with holes, and stained with soot.

"It's not that bad," I said. "We've still got the important part." I pointed to the gray-and-purple swath of the bayou, with the twisted thorn mark at its center. I bent closer, taking note of the rather large number of unpleasant illustrations scattered across the page. And that didn't even count the ones that were burned away.

Well, I didn't expect it was going to be easy. But at least with this map we had some hope of navigating. "We just need to get here." I pointed to a red spot on the rim of a blackened hole. "That town's the closest we can get, right where the Sangue runs into the bayou." I squinted, trying to make out the name. "Something's Edge, I think it says. There, next to the picture of the funny-looking house."

"Veil's Edge," Barnaby said. "And that's a paddle-boat, not a house. We'll take the western highway. Get there in less than a week, which is good, since I don't fancy being out on the road for the Night of a Thousand Frights."

I sighed, lowering my head into my hands. The rice and sausage had lost their savor. "So we're fine as long as I don't accidentally burn down every town between here and Veil's Edge."

"Don't look so glum," said Barnaby. "For what it's worth, you did terrify the poor shopkeeper. Wouldn't your granny be pleased with that? Striking fear into the hearts of the Uplanders and all?" He refilled my cup of tea and pushed it toward me. The spicy steam stung my eyes. "That flaming green inferno spell was brill—"

"I don't need your sympathy," I snapped.

Barnaby leaned back. "Right. Bog-witches don't need help, or praise, or a kind word, or any of that stuff."

I did, though. That was the worst part. But Barnaby wasn't my grandmother. He was probably just trying to be charming. I fumed silently.

"I, on the other hand, quite enjoyed it," Barnaby went on. He produced a gold coin from somewhere and balanced it on the tip of one finger, making it spin, dazzling me with glittering flashes.

"You mean you enjoyed the gold coins and the new clothes."

"I won't say I didn't. But . . ." Barnaby caught the coin and tucked it away. He looked into the distance. "It felt . . . good, I guess. When they all thanked me. To have everyone crowding around like that, thinking I was someone fine and noble." Then he grinned. "You see, you ought to try kindness and courtesy. They'll get you more in the end."

I set down my teacup. "So, when you say nice things, it's only to get what you want? Like when you said those things about me—about my spells, I mean. You didn't really mean it. It was no different from tipping your hat to some girl on the street. You were just being polite." I felt oddly raw, like a freshly shucked clam.

Barnaby groaned. "I *did* mean it. But, filthy fens, I don't know why I'm bothering. It's flipping crazy to try to make friends with a bog-witch." He looked away, toward the front of the inn.

Friends. The word twanged inside me. What should I say? I opened my mouth to tell him I didn't need friends, but nothing came out.

This was ridiculous. It was probably just too much molasses pie. "I'm going to my room," I said, finally. I needed some time alone. I could practice my curses— or maybe not. I did rather look forward to sleeping in the goose-feather bed, and it would be a shame if it got accidentally toasted.

I had half risen from the bench when Barnaby gave a strangled yelp.

"What?" I said, looking toward the front of the inn. I didn't see anything unusual. The grim innkeeper was wiping out mugs and glowering at the smoldering fire. Several people hunched around the bar, listening to a woman telling a tale in between puffs on her long pipe.

Then I noticed him. A tall man in a long gray coat, his face shadowed by a wide-brimmed hat. Perfectly nondescript, yet once I saw him I had trouble pulling my gaze away. The man leaned across the bar, speaking to the innkeeper. Something under the brim of his hat glinted.

"Barnaby, do you know— Barnaby?" I stared at the empty bench on the other side of the table. Where had he gotten to? And how had he left the table without my noticing?

"Shhh!" came a hiss from somewhere near my feet. I started to bend down.

"No, don't move!" Barnaby whispered. "He'll see."

I set my elbows back on the table. "Who is he?"

"Filthy fens, I've got to get out of here . . . What's he doing now?"

"He's got some sort of scroll," I said, observing the man over the rim of my teacup. "He's showing it to the innkeeper."

"Blast him to the pits. Why can't he leave me alone? Prunella, you've got to distract him. If he sees me—"

"He's looking this way."

Barnaby scuttled deeper into the shadows under the table, pressing himself back against the wall.

"It's all right, he's not coming over."

"Not yet."

"Why don't you just try kindness and courtesy?"

"If you knew what he's done . . . Oh, forget it. You're probably enjoying this."

All my sarcasm drained away. I could hear the edge

of fear in Barnaby's voice. I squinted again at the man in the gray coat. He was speaking to the pipe-smoking woman now. My breath caught as he lifted his head. He had a lean, hunting, hungry look. Set in one eye was a round gold-rimmed lens. I squinted and caught a shimmer in the air.

"That monocle," I gasped. "It's enchanted. Who is he?"

Barnaby groaned unhelpfully.

Whoever he was, it was clear that sooner or later he would make his way to our corner. I didn't think even Barnaby could remain hidden then. He was right. We needed a diversion. I rubbed my sticky fingers together thoughtfully, looking toward the hearth. Fire had betrayed me. Perhaps smoke would serve me better.

"Do you think you could find your way out of here if you couldn't see?"

"Why? I mean, yes, I'll go for that door to the kitchens, then out the back. There's an alley beside the stables."

"I'll meet you there," I said, furling the map and tucking it away. Then I drained the last of my tea, stood up, and marched to the hearth.

"You there," said a cold voice behind me. "Have you seen this boy?"

I hurried my steps, pretending I had not heard his question or seen the curling parchment he held out. I caught the flash of a single word—WANTED—inscribed above a drawing of a boy who looked very much like Barnaby, although with longer hair.

Was Barnaby indeed a criminal? I trembled, half of me wanting to turn back, to ask a hundred questions. But there was no time, not if I wanted to gain Esmeralda's grimoire. That was all that truly mattered.

I knelt beside the fire. Ashes drifted across the wide stones. I swept my sticky fingers through the fine gray powder. The thunk of boot heels told me I didn't have long. I took a deep breath.

A steely hand seized my shoulder, pulling me around just as I finished muttering the incantation. "You do not walk away from an official of the queen, girl."

I stared up into his brilliant blue eyes, pitiless as a clear winter sky. The golden rim of the monocle circumscribed my world for a brief, endless moment. My hands felt as if they were caught in ice, unable to finish the last gesture to complete my spell.

Then his blue gaze slipped down, taking in my ashy fingers, the chicken foot that had worked its way free to dangle openly yet again. "A bog-witch?" His mouth fell open. Now he was the one with fear in his eyes. I twitched my fingers.

The next moment, swirls of thick black smoke filled the inn. The hands gripping my shoulders loosened. I wrenched away.

Shouts of alarm filled my ears. Thuds and grunts and wails echoed through the choking blackness. I threw myself down, creeping along the floor in the direction of the front door.

Once outside, I scrambled to my feet and ducked around back to find Barnaby coughing and sputtering, his white collar dark with soot. We didn't stop running until the tallest towers of Withywatch had fallen below the horizon.

Chapter 4

"The first thing I'm going to do when we get to Sweet-water is find a tea shop and drink three mugs of iced hot-leaf," said Barnaby, running one hand across his forehead. "Then a nap. No," he said, looking down at himself, "then a bath, then a nap." He shook his head. "I didn't get half so grubbed when I was—" He stopped. "That is, this adventuring business makes it hard for a fellow to stay presentable."

"You look perfectly fine," I said. "And well you should, after I used up all my soapstone on that cleans-ing charm." I had been rather pleased with how well it had worked. Between that and the smoke I'd sum-moned at the Tipsy Coon, I was feeling considerably more confident. "But you could go back and have a drink and a wash at that spring I found."

Barnaby made a choking noise. "That water was half mud. We're too close to the Bottomlands."

"It tasted fine to me," I said. "Green and alive, like the bog." In fact, I'd lingered there far longer than necessary, breathing in the damp air, thinking of home. I had already used up my ginger leaves and the pyre root and all the soapstone, and I'd only been in the Uplands for two days. The bland patchwork of green and gold fields dragged at me. I made myself dizzy staring, searching for a hint of magic. But there was none. We might be close to the Bottomlands, but I was in an alien world.

"Green like pond scum," Barnaby said. "I'll wait till we reach the village. I hear they've got the best well in the Uplands. Folks come from all around to drink the water. They say it's magic and it'll cure anything that ails you."

Somehow I doubted an enchanted well would give me warts and make my curses work properly. But I was looking forward to a rest, and something to fill my belly. We'd been tramping along the western highway for hours, after a restless night camped out in a cornfield, with Barnaby jumping up at every little rustle, convinced the man with the enchanted monocle had found him.

No matter how I wheedled and pried, the most I could get out of Barnaby was that the monocle let the man see things beyond normal sight: magic and enchantments and spirits. He refused to tell me anything about why the fellow was pursuing him, and I abandoned the effort when he became grouchy.

Now that we were well on our way, walking under a cloudless blue sky through the green meadows, Barnaby had regained his airy cheer. Perhaps a bit too much cheer.

"Do you always whistle?" I asked.

"What's wrong with whistling?"

What was wrong was that his silly little tune made my steps bounce, as if I were trotting across billowing clouds. I felt ridiculous. Who ever heard of a bog-witch skipping along past meadows full of daisies and coneflowers? I forced my feet into a more appropriate stalking gait.

"There, I see smoke." Barnaby pointed toward a gap in the thicket of oaks that ran along the next rise. I was about to follow when I spied something else, above the oaks. Three black forms flapping through the air, circling above the highway.

"What is it?" Barnaby asked.

"Nothing." I forced myself to keep going. "The crows."

"Crows? What, some sort of bog-witch bad omen?"

"No. My grandmother likes them. She even has this

crow-skin spell where she can turn herself into one. And remember that charm in the asparagus bed?"

"For the rest of my life, thank you very much. But there must be thousands of crows in the world. Not to mention that we're in the Uplands."

"The charm would still work if she created the skin in the Bottomlands," I said. "But you're probably right. She did throw me out."

She wouldn't bother keeping an eye on me, I told myself. Would she?

One of the birds swooped down, cawing raucously over my head. It winged away to join the others, who now perched in the branches above. As we passed beneath, beady black eyes fixed upon me. I wondered what Grandmother would think if she heard I was traveling around with a boy set on recovering the lost chalice and becoming the hero of the Uplands.

By the time we reached the first cottages of Sweetwater, the crows were nothing but distant black specks. I didn't have long to ponder whether I felt glad or sad that they hadn't followed me.

"Something's wrong," said Barnaby. He'd stopped whistling as we passed into the central square.

"What?" I glanced around, taking in the cheerful whitewashed buildings with striped awnings, the large stone urns decorating the street corners. "It's not your friend with the magic monocle again?"

"He's *not* my friend. And with any luck he's still a day behind us." He gestured around us. "But look at the people. They look . . . afraid. And there should be more of them. And what's with the flowers?"

We had just passed by one of the urns. A scruff of withered brown protruded from the top. A single faded trumpet flower hung sadly from the dead vine. I stared across the street to where two men hunched, talking in low, grumbling voices. An old woman hustled past, her dark cloak shielding the two small children at her side.

"There's a tea shop," said Barnaby. "Come on."

The sign above the red-striped awning showed a jaunty blue teacup, but from the looks of the place, no one was drinking much hot-leaf here. The proprietor was a leathery-faced woman with her hair tied back so tightly it made my own head hurt to look at her. Barnaby, of course, turned on his charm as he swaggered forward between the empty tables.

"Kind lady, might I prevail upon you for an iced hot-leaf? I've heard such tales of the brews here at the Blue Cup. I've been longing to sample them."

To Barnaby's credit, she did smile. But it was a weak, pitiful thing that did not reach her eyes. "I wish

I might oblige you, lad. But there'll be no more tea in all Sweetwater, not until the curse is put to rights."

"The curse of the stolen chalice?" said Barnaby. Two spots of crimson lit his cheeks.

"That very one. Ever since the Mirable Chalice was stolen, misfortunes have been our lot here in Sweetwater. The seeds rot in the fields. Folk are struck down with the wasting. And worst of all, the well's gone bad."

"Bad? You mean it's dried up?" Barnaby slumped onto a stool at one of the tables.

She shook her head. "The water's poison. It tastes as foul as fens, and it's as dark as night. You see how the flowers take to it." She gestured to the urn. "And so there's not a drop of tea in all Sweetwater. Just a bit of milk, all the goats can manage. Would you like some? Or I've a bit of last year's cider to spare. We haven't had many visitors lately, not since word of the curse got round. It's a real pleasure to have you here, young Master . . . ?" She trailed off questioningly.

"Barnaby, just Barnaby," he said, smiling and slipping a silver coin onto the table. "And I'll have some of your cider, please." He looked to me.

The proprietor followed his gaze. She frowned. "I beg your pardon, Master Barnaby. Is this person a friend of yours?"

Barnaby mumbled something noncommittal. I

forced a smile onto my lips, thinking of pitchforks and torches. "Ah . . . um . . . hello . . ."

The sight of the woman's face turned my words to stone. Her lip had curled. Over her shoulder, Barnaby mouthed the words "chicken foot." Blast the thing, it had gotten loose again! I tucked it under my scarf and plowed onward. "Prunella Bogthistle." I dipped a sort of half-bow, the best I could manage.

"Bog . . . thistle? A Bottomlander?"

"There's nothing wrong with the Bottomlands," I said, fire coming into my voice and into my heart.

She stepped back a pace, passing her hand across her eyes, warding against evil. "A bog-witch," she spat. "So you've come to add to our suffering, have you?"

I wanted to turn and run back to that spring that had smelled like green living things, but what sort of bog-witch would I be then? Grandmother would never let some Uplander say such things. I drew myself up tall and haughty, wishing I knew a curse that would drive that horrible look from the woman's face.

"No need for alarm, fair lady," said Barnaby, stepping between us. "Prunella's from the Bottomlands, yes, but she's . . . um . . . a good bog-witch. She's . . . here to lift the curse. With me. We're traveling together." It seemed to cost him some effort to get the words out, but he grinned at me afterward.

I stared at him. The tea-shop proprietress pursed her lips, raking a doubtful glance over me. "All well and good, lad. But we don't want any more trouble here. We've troubles enough without her sort coming round."

Barnaby pulled me down onto the stool beside him, giving my elbow a tweak as he did so. "Just play along," he whispered. Then, more loudly, "We're on a quest for the lost chalice. And we will gladly do all we can to aid you in lifting this curse from your well."

The woman sniffed. She stepped back behind her counter, then returned with two cups. She set one before Barnaby, brimming with cider. The other she deposited beside me. I peered into it, just able to make out the glimmer of liquid down at the bottom. Fine. So much for kindness and courtesy.

"So the well has been cursed for a while now?" Barnaby asked, after he'd drained half his cup.

The woman nodded. "It's been three months, and there's many who say we ought to pack up and leave. But it's only the chalice that's kept doom from the Uplands all these years. If it's gone, where can we go? Nowhere will be safe if the evils of the bog rise up against us again." She narrowed her eyes, looking at me.

Barnaby drummed his fingers on the table. His hand drifted down to his pack, lying beside him on the ground. He tossed back the last of his cider and set the cup down with a thump. "Let's take a look at this cursed well."

The tea-shop mistress pointed toward the center of the town square. "It's there."

I squinted against the sun toward the raised stone platform. Barnaby stood, shouldering his pack. "Come on, Prunella." Without waiting for my reply, he set off toward the well.

I hurried after him. "So now you believe there's a curse? I thought you said it was just sniffles and corn rot."

"You saw that tailor in Withywatch. That was no sniffle, and it bothered you as much as it did me, so don't try playing the heartless bog-witch."

"I liked her clothes, that's all." I jigged from foot to foot, the memory of Mary Morland's desperate eyes haunting me even now. "Anyway, this probably has nothing to do with that."

"Or maybe it's all connected. We've got to try, at least." Barnaby seized the handle of the heavy oaken round that covered the well. The wood scraped back across the stones, exposing a dark, dank pit. He looked at me, a strange intensity in his gaze. "So. What do you think? Is it cursed?"

"If it is, maybe they deserve it," I muttered. I could still feel the tea woman staring at me from under her awning. But there were others watching us now, too.

Hollow-eyed women and nervous men, and a scattering of children with overbright eyes and overeager smiles. I sighed. I might as well check it out.

I circled the well and ran my fingers across the stones. Slitting my eyes, I saw nothing but the thistles and crescents carved into the worn granite. "That's odd," I said, tracing the carvings with my finger. "It looks as if the well was charmed once. Standard stuff—keep out the critters, purify the water, make sure it stays full. But it's gone. I can't see a speck of magic left."

"Then it's not cursed?" Barnaby expelled the breath he'd been holding.

"I don't know. There's something strange . . ." I leaned out over the darkness, sniffing, then listening. Below the glopping of the water, I thought I caught a faint throbbing drone, like a fat bullfrog.

I scrambled away from the edge and clutched my chicken foot. Barnaby drew his dagger, moving to stand between me and the well. "Are you all right? Is it the curse?"

"I'm fine," I panted. "There's no curse. But we should leave. Now." I took a step back, my fingers tight around my withered talisman, tensed for any sound from the depths of the well.

"If it's not cursed, why do you look like you just ran smack into a swamp ghoul?"

"That's not far off," I said. "I'd rather a swamp ghoul than a pondswaggle." I swallowed, but the lump in my throat remained. "Let's go, Barnaby. Before it notices us."

"Wait." The boy stood his ground. "You're saying the water's gone bad because some swamp demon's shacked up down there?"

I nodded, inching back another step.

"Could the protection charm have lost its magic because the chalice was stolen?"

"I don't know. Maybe. Or maybe it just faded away. The charm must have been put there more than two hundred years ago. But it doesn't matter! It's gone now, and the pondswaggle's moved in, and *we* need to leave."

"We've got to get that thing out. I told these folks we'd help them." Barnaby gripped his dagger more tightly.

"Fine, you get it out, then. I didn't promise anything."

"How bad is it, really?" Barnaby asked. "I've never even heard of a pondswaggle. It can't be as bad as a wraith or a gargarou or a spectral stallion."

"One of them chased me and my cousin Ezzie halfway across the Swamp of Shivers just because she called it a toad. We only got away because we hid in a leech pit." I squirmed at the memory. "Ezzie couldn't stop it, and her curses actually *work*. What do you expect me to do?"

"I don't know." Barnaby let out a long huff, running his hands back through his untidy hair. "But you've got a better shot than these folks. Come on, you heard the tea lady's story. It might not look like a curse, but it started when the chalice went missing. We have to help them."

"I don't see why you're so keen to play the hero. These aren't the sort who are going to shower you with gold when you're done."

He ignored me. He picked up the bucket standing nearby, then tugged on the rope that connected it to a thick iron ring set into the stones. "I'm going down to kill that thing. With or without your help."

"Go down there and you'll just get yourself killed. And it'll be your own fault for being an idiot." I turned around, trying not to notice the large crowd of people who had gathered on the edges of the plaza.

"You know, I started to think that you might not be half bad, Prunella," said Barnaby. "That maybe you weren't just another Esmeralda. I guess I was wrong."

I was going to walk away. I was. Grandmother would have marched out of that town without a backward look. But the chains clanked, and terrible images of sharp teeth tearing into Barnaby filled my mind.

"Wait!" I took a step back toward the well. My

insides felt like a cloud of needlewings. "You can't go down there. It'll kill you!"

He paused, one foot in the bucket. "And you can't bear to live without me?"

I sniffed. "I need you, that's all. To get Esmeralda's grimoire. So I suppose I have to help you. You can't take on the pondswaggle with just that." I nodded at his dagger. "Ezzie hit the one chasing us with the biggest fireball she could and didn't even singe its eyelashes. We can't fight it."

Barnaby took his foot out of the bucket and crossed his arms. "I'm listening. What do you suggest?"

"We lead it far enough away that it won't be able to find its way back." At least not until after we were long gone from Sweetwater. I didn't tell him that part. "We just need to get it angry and it'll chase us anywhere."

"Wonderful," said Barnaby, peering doubtfully into the well. "So we're bait." An especially loud burbling rose from the depths just then. The boy wrinkled his nose. "I'm not hiding in a leech pit, though. I'd rather try my luck against the pondswaggle."

He looked around the plaza. I shivered under the press of so many eyes.

"Don't they have anything better to do?" I muttered. "Do they have to stare?"

Barnaby gave the crowds a cheery wave. "People of Sweetwater," he proclaimed, "have no fear. We will cleanse the curse from your fair well." A ragged spate of applause broke out, led by the woman from the tea shop.

"We must summon the terrible beast that lurks below and lure it from the town," Barnaby went on. "Please, keep back!"

"Are you finished showing off?" I said, after he joined me again at the edge of the well.

"Oh, don't be sour. Don't they look like they could use cheering up? Besides, it will make for a better show when we come back victo— Ugh! Not that thing again."

I had just pulled the chicken foot out from under my scarf. I smirked. "You see, it's a good thing I kept this around. Pondswaggles hate chickens." I reached out over the well. Cold air raised gooseflesh along my arms and back. I tried not to think about running across the Swamp of Shivers, and Ezzie's squeals, and the gurgling bellows of the pondswaggle. My heart hammered so hard I thought it might burst.

I dropped the chicken foot. A moment later, a *sploosh* echoed up from the well. Then a grumble rose, growing louder by the moment. I tugged Barnaby back from the lip of the well just as a spout of fetid water spurted up. A warty green creature leapt from the plume and goggled at us with froggy eyes. A stench worse than a pot of eel soup gone bad washed over us. Barnaby gulped, but stood his ground. My own pride kept me in place, though my feet itched to run.

"Who did that?" demanded the pondswaggle. "What ragscrabble dunderhead dared profane my home?"

Screams and shouts rose from the edges of the plaza. I caught a flurry of motion as the crowd scattered. Barnaby didn't seem able to move. I supposed the stench was too much for his Uplander nose.

"I did," I croaked. I licked my lips. I had to work quickly, before I lost my nerve. "Not much of a home, is it, Barnaby? No place you'd find a real pondswaggle. A well? In the Uplands?"

The goggle-eyed creature glared up at me for a long moment. I twitched my toes, ready to dash for the road the moment it came after us.

Then a great fat tear slipped from one of the pondswaggle's eyes and rolled down his green cheek. "You're right," he said, in a voice that sounded as if it were fighting its way up out from under ten feet of mud. "I'm *not* a real pondswaggle."

"What?" I remained tensed to run, in case this was some sort of trick.

"Look at me," glugged the creature, waving bulbous fingertips at himself. "A real pondswaggle wouldn't be living in a well, stinking of charms, surrounded by stones and people who throw chicken feet on him." He slumped down onto the edge of the well. "But I didn't have anywhere else to go . . ." He fell into a long soggy fit of tears.

"Oh, it can't be that bad," I said. I couldn't believe I was actually feeling sorry for a pondswaggle. But the thought of the poor thing wandering in the unmagical Uplands raised an echoing ache inside me. I searched for something useful to say. "You look like a real pondswaggle. What's your name?"

He gulped. "P-pogboggen."

"See, that's a fine pondswagglish name. Right, Barnaby? Isn't Pog here the most impressive pondswaggle you've ever seen?"

"Um . . . yes. Of course. The greenest, the swaggliest." Barnaby dug in his pocket and produced a square of green silk. He offered it to Pog between the tips of his fingers.

The creature buried his nose in the handkerchief and let out a long, despairing honk. "My brother has a fen all his own, right in the middle of the Bogthistle demesne. He's so terrible he once chased two bog-witches across the Swamp of Shivers. And my sister has the entire moat at Blackthorn Manor all to herself." He rubbed a knobbly hand across his wet eyes. "And then there's me, not a soggy spot to call my own, wandering high and dry. The best I could do was a stinking old well still itchy with wards. And in the middle of a town! In the Uplands! It's no wonder they never come and visit. They despise me."

"Oh." I hastily rearranged my thoughts. "So, if there was a nice, green-smelling spring with a little bit of a pool nearby, would that be better?"

The pondswaggle's face split into a wide smile. I tried not to shudder at the rows of sharp teeth. "A pool? That's almost a pond, isn't it?"

"That's right," said Barnaby. "And it'll really be a pond, once there's a pondswaggle living in it."

"It's just back a ways, down the road to the east." I pointed.

The pondswaggle blinked. "You can show me where it is?"

"Of course," said Barnaby, warming to the plot.

The froggy creature leapt away. Shrieks and yells rose from those denizens of Sweetwater who had not yet retreated. The onlookers scrambled back, clearing the path out of town.

Barnaby raised his arms. "People of Sweetwater . . ."

I didn't wait to hear his speech. I had to run to keep

up with the pondswaggle's great bounding pace. He would dash ahead, nearly disappearing behind the rises in the road, before rushing back to ask how far it was.

This was almost as bad as my flight across the Swamp of Shivers. By the time Barnaby caught up with me, I had a burning stitch in my side and was gulping down air like a half-drowned rat.

"Nearly there," I told Pog when he returned for the dozenth time. "Just ahead. Around that bend and between the two boulders." I paused, trying to catch my breath.

"I can smell it!" The pondswaggle bounded onward gleefully.

"You think this will work?" asked Barnaby, jogging up to join me.

A shrill cry of delight echoed back to us, followed by a *sploosh*!

"I think it already has."

"What about the well?"

"It ought to clear up quickly, now that he's out," I said. "But even then, it'll still just be water. Like I said, the charms are gone."

Barnaby nodded. For a moment we stood listening to the joyful hooting and hollering coming from the spring. Barnaby grinned. "We didn't do half bad, did we?"

"We?" I raised one brow.

"Fine, fine. You did most of it. Though I'd never have guessed you could be so . . ."

"What?"

"If I say 'kind and courteous,' are you going to try to curse me again?"

I pursed my lips. "His brother and sister should have visited him, even if he was in a well. Or they should have let him live with them in their fens and ponds."

"So you felt sorry for him?"

I did. But I wasn't going to say anything more to Barnaby about it. "Let's go back. The Mistveil isn't getting any closer."

We bade our farewells to Pogboggen, declining his invitation to stay for tea. He wasn't a bad sort, after all, but tea with a pondswaggle seemed a chancy affair, especially after hearing Pog's raptures over the quality of the flies buzzing around the pool. Still, we promised to return when we could, and eventually he allowed us to continue on our way.

Walking back toward Sweetwater, my feet sprang as if the highway were clouds underfoot, even though Barnaby wasn't whistling. Twice I even caught myself smiling.

"Hurry up, Prunella," called Barnaby, several paces ahead. He had just reached the top of the ridge beneath the oaks. "They'll probably want to have a feast. I can smell the roast already!" He hastened down the other side, heading for the village.

Before I could follow, a raucous croaking drew my gaze upward. Three crows circled above. My feet turned to stone, locking me there, in the shadow of the tree.

I stood unmoving as the cheers roared up from the town. I could hear cries of "Barnaby! Barnaby the hero!"

Still I stood there. What was I doing? Was I really racing off after cheers and adulation? I gazed up at the crows. Then I walked forward, just enough so I could peer down past the bole of the tree, to Sweetwater.

It looked as if every single person in town had come out to line the highway. I saw a figure in a green jacket being propelled along through the crowd. I squinted. Was he looking back? Searching the hillside? Wondering where I was?

Or was he only turning to take in the riot of cheers all the better?

Blast it. If he wanted to go off without me, fine. I didn't need any stinking cheers. I glared up at the circling crows, then headed off into the woody scrub. I would go around the town. Barnaby could find me on the other side, once he tired of being cheered and fêted and feasted. By then, I hoped, I would have banished this choking tight feeling in my throat and the wretched stinging in my eyes.

I had a camp all prepared by the time Barnaby found me. A fire snapped, roasting a skewer of mushrooms and two ears of straggly corn I'd nicked from one of the Sweetwater fields. I figured that they owed me that much, at least.

"I'm surprised you didn't stay in town," I said as he joined me beside the fire. "Didn't the mayor offer you his feather bed? Weren't there enough girls with ribbons in their hair bringing you hot-leaf and sugar biscuits?"

"I was more in the mood for roasted mushrooms anyway," he said, breathing in the aroma of the skewers appreciatively.

"Oh. Well, fine. I suppose you can stay here."

"If you didn't think I'd be back, why did you pile up two beds of rushes?"

I sniffed. "Maybe I shouldn't have. You'll ruin your fancy clothes, and I already used up all my soapstone."

"No worries, the worthy folk of Sweetwater gave me a new set." Barnaby held up a rich purple coat and pristine white shirt. He even had a jaunty new cap to match.

"I don't suppose they gave you anything practical?"

"Of course. Two blankets, a packet of hot-leaf, a flask of Sweetwater sweetwater, and some very fine sausages. It's not bad being the hero."

I glowered into the fire as he set his pack over by one of the trees.

"They would have cheered you, too, you know, if you hadn't run away," he said after a moment.

"I don't need cheers. I need to get to the Mistveil."

"Oh," said Barnaby, returning to the fire, "I do have something for you."

I lifted my head, my heart thudding strangely. Then I saw what he was holding out. My chicken foot.

"They found it while they were clearing the muck out of the well. I figured you'd want it back."

I snatched it out of his hand. "I'll be sure to keep it out of sight."

Barnaby gave an exasperated sigh. "I'm going to go get more firewood. You can sit there glooming, or you can do something useful, like cooking the sausages." He jerked his thumb back toward the tree. "You got exactly what you wanted, Prunella, so stop being such a prickly shrew about it."

He tramped off into the woods before I could come up with a response. Which was just as well, since I probably would have tried to curse him. Or burst into tears.

Barnaby was a means to an end, I reminded myself. I didn't need him to like me. I needed him to get me into Blackthorn's treasury, so I could get the grimoire and go back to the Bottomlands, where things made sense and I knew who I was. I had to stay focused.

And I wasn't going to sit around glooming about it. I pushed myself up and headed over to the tree where Barnaby's sack lay. He'd hung his new jacket from one of the branches. I disdained the silly gilt-embroidered thing and knelt beside the pack, setting my hand on the buckle.

"What do you think you're doing?"

I jerked upright at the harsh demand. Barnaby strode forward, tossing an armful of wood beside the fire. The sticks clattered and bounced, throwing up sparks as they knocked against the burning logs.

"Trying to do something useful," I retorted. "You said I should cook the sausages!"

He snatched up the pack, his eyes flicking over the buckle. I hadn't even worked the tongue out. "The sausages are right there," he said, jabbing a finger at the tree.

Looking up, I saw several brown links dangling from another branch, beside Barnaby's coat. "I didn't see them," I said. "I thought they were in your pack. It's heavy enough one might think you were carrying all the sausages in the Uplands! And now you're yelling at me when I was just trying to—to help."

Barnaby stared at me. He seemed to be breathing too quickly. Then he thumped himself down beside the fire, setting aside his cap and running fingers back through his disheveled hair. "I'm sorry for snapping at you, Prunella. I guess I'm . . . I keep thinking about the Sweetwater well. You said it wasn't cursed. But what could make the charm stop working like that? Maybe it *is* because the chalice was stolen. There's three more taken ill here, just like that tailor in Withywatch." He let out a gusty sigh.

I scrambled for something to say. "There's no point worrying about it now. You did everything you could. I was the one who wanted to leave."

"You're not the one calling himself a hero," Barnaby said dourly.

"Still. We did help them. The Sweetwater people and Pogboggen, both. You remember *Secrets of the Mistveil*? It said something about breaking the curse. Maybe when we get to Blackthorn Manor we'll also find out how to fix this mess."

Barnaby grunted. "And how many more charms d'you reckon will fail before that? How many more folks'll get sick with this blasted wasting?" He drummed his fingers against his pack, brooding. "Maybe I ought to . . ."

"What?" I prompted. I narrowed my eyes. "Does it have something to do with that man in the monocle?"

"No!" Barnaby replied. "Let's eat and get some rest. We've got a long way to go yet."

Chapter 5

We spent the next week making our way west across the Uplands. It should only have taken three days at the most, but Barnaby insisted on following several odd roundabout routes. I suspected he was attempting to evade the man with the enchanted monocle.

Avoiding pursuit was not the only thing that slowed us down. In every settlement we passed through, we found more tales of woe. Crops dying, illness, injury, and fire. They called it a curse; I didn't know what to call it. I saw weathered carvings that had once held wards, wood that still hummed with the memory of old enchantments. In one village they thought they were cursed with baldness, when really it was just a very powerful hair-growing charm that had stopped working.

I had to do something. I knew Grandmother wouldn't approve; I'd heard enough of her lectures on the evils of magical do-gooding. But she was still holed up in the Bottomlands, and I was out here, looking at the thin faces, staring into the desperate eyes. So I did what I could. We both did, Barnaby and I. Sometimes it wasn't much. In the balding village, Barnaby's only contribution was to give the barber some much-needed business. In other places, I made good use of my alligator-spoor curse, and we chased out several run-of-the-mill bog-varmints.

I never stayed for the cheering. But one time a little girl caught me ducking out the back gate and gave me a shy smile and a pumpkin tart. It was the tastiest thing I'd ever eaten. Even better than fried bread.

Some ills we could not cure. Everywhere we went, we found folk struck down with the wasting. Many were laid up in beds, like the Withywatch tailor. Others still managed a semblance of life, listlessly chopping carrots or watching with hollow eyes as I tried to charm away the mysterious ailment, to no avail. They were as dull as weathered winter grasses, when they should have been fresh and green with life. It was as if their will to live was sapping away. But where had it gone? And why?

The hardest part was when Barnaby talked about the Mirable Chalice. He asked me every day how much longer I thought it would be until we reached Blackthorn

Manor. I supposed he was torn between stopping to help, and hurrying on to find the chalice and end the curse once and for all.

That was when I started thinking about what he would say if he broke through all the wards and locks and traps into Blackthorn's treasury and discovered there was no chalice. Grandmother thought it was there, but did she know for certain? What if I'd led Barnaby on a fool's errand? When I started out, my daydreams were all of the grimoire, of what it might look like, of the secrets it might contain. Of how it would feel to hold it in my hands. Like a proper bog-witch, I'd thought only of my own ends.

But I wasn't a proper bog-witch anymore. I could feel it slipping away, with every smile I caught fleeting across my lips, with every feather and frond I pulled from my braids to help one of the beleaguered villages. I still missed the music of the frogs and the chatter of my aunts and the pulsing, buzzing life of the bog. Yet each day I shed more of my magic, and I was desperately afraid I was losing myself along with it.

I knew something had changed when Barnaby returned to our night's camp to offer me a handful of cranberries and a jar of honey. "A taste of home," he said, flashing me a smile.

A month ago, my heart would never have given

that odd little leap at such a gift. I clamped down on the feeling. I had to get that grimoire and return to the bog, before something worse happened. I held up my hands, warding the gift away. Barnaby's face fell. "I'm a horrible cook," I protested. "Truly! You'll never want to look at cranberries again. But thank you. For finding them." He still looked as if I'd trampled on his prize mushroom patch. I relented. "Here, then, you stew them up, and I'll go get corn to make fritters."

"It's a deal," he said, grinning. "Only—"

"What?"

"Be careful."

"The Night of a Thousand Frights isn't until tomorrow. And besides, I know how to deal with frights. I am from the Bottomlands, you know."

He nodded, still looking uneasily into the woods around us. "I just feel like something's watching."

I double-checked the branches above, remembering the crows from Sweetwater. Nothing. I headed off for the corn.

It was while I was walking back with my scarf full of corncobs that I made my decision. Well, actually, it was while I was walking back that I discovered a nice lot of mushrooms growing down the side of a culvert, and while I was picking them I found the old stump full of water that was just right for a finding charm.

Since I couldn't banish my worries with force of will, I would just have to do something to find out for sure where the stinking chalice was. The stump was perfect, and even though I'd never actually done a finding spell, I was pretty sure I could replicate Aunt Flywell's gestures. There was only one problem.

Twitching my braid forward, I fingered the tassels of flame grass I'd woven into it. The feathery grass was the last bit of the Bottomlands I had left. Even my chicken foot was several days gone, spent on an attempt to recharm an enchanted soup pot.

I untwisted the crackling reddish frond, trying not to notice how my fingers trembled. I forced myself not to slit my gaze. I knew well enough what I would see. A shimmering handful of dried grass, and a dull, dull world all around. I still had my talent, of course, but I was a scribe with one last drop of ink. Was I really about to spend that last drop on Barnaby? I clutched the flame grass in my hand. Once this was gone, who would I be? Could I even call myself a bog-witch?

I didn't have to do this. The chalice didn't matter to me. Only the grimoire, the key to my future as a bog-witch.

I thought of the girl who had given me that tart, of Mary Morland and her hungry eyes. I thought of Barnaby, how fierce and determined he'd looked, standing on the edge of the well in Sweetwater. I thought of Pogboggen. Wasn't he still a pondswaggle? Even living in a well, or a spring? I opened my fingers, letting the flame grass fall into the water-filled stump. I let out my breath in a long whoosh.

I wove my hands through the air the way Aunt Flywell had. For lack of any better incantation, I whispered, "Please, show me where the Mirable Chalice is. For Barnaby. For the Uplands. For me, and not just so I won't feel guilty."

The grass quivered. I stared at it, willing it to move, to point in the direction of the Mirable Chalice. Slowly, slowly, it started to drift, then to spin, the red tips shifting from south, to southeast, to east . . . It was working! Now north, now northwest. I held my breath. The Mistveil lay to the southwest. Perhaps I had been right all along!

The grass spun to the southwest and kept going. I stared as it continued to spin, like the spoke of a wheel, round and round. A curl of smoke rose from it. Then— with a hollow *poof!*—the entire frond sizzled, spat, and sputtered to a crisp.

Blast it! I snatched up the blackened flame grass and tossed it aside. I was no better at this than I was at cursing. I bowed my head, wanting to weep. I'd used my last bit of magic on a foolish, stupid attempt to help people, and of course it had backfired. I ran my fingers through my hair, missing the weight of the ornaments and trinkets.

The thud of running feet jerked me from my despair. I leapt up. Barnaby hurtled out of the undergrowth, his face flushed.

"Sweet hills," he panted. "Finally." Barnaby shoved his pack at me. My corncobs and mushrooms fell to the ground. "Hide it!" Barnaby whispered. "He's here!"

"Who? What? Barnaby, I—"

"Barnaby Bagby!" called a voice. I whirled around, trying to tell which direction it had come from. Chills raced up and down my arms. I knew that voice. The man with the enchanted monocle.

"Who is he?" I demanded. "Why is he looking for you?"

"Please, Prunella. Just do it."

There was no jaunty grin, no sure smile. Only fear and desperation. I nodded. He ran, crashing away through the bushes as if he were trying to get every hunter in the Uplands after him.

I stood there for a moment, until the cold voice called out again. Now it seemed to be coming from the direction Barnaby had run in. He was leading the man away from me. No, away from the pack. Realization began to work its way through my thoughts.

I unbuckled the flap and peered inside. Out of the pack came his spare green jacket, the flask, a single copper penny, and . . .

A gleaming golden chalice.

I'd never heard a description of the Mirable Chalice, but I had a strong suspicion that it was about the length of my forearm, delicately wrought and etched with vines and flowers. Exactly like the chalice I held in my hand. I squinted, then yelped at the blaze of magic that filled my vision. I had never seen an enchantment this strong.

My spell hadn't flopped. It had shown me exactly where the chalice was, even as Barnaby ran through the woods like a crazed thing looking for me. But there my thoughts battered into a wall, unable to make sense of it. Why was Barnaby on a quest for the Mirable Chalice if he already had it?

"You can't run forever, Barnaby," called the man with the monocle. "I know you stole it, like the thief you are. You will pay for what you've done."

A strangled cry echoed through the woods, breaking my daze into sharp-edged fear. Whoever the man with the monocle was, he had Barnaby, and meant to do him ill. I had to help him. But what good was I with all my trinkets and alchemy now gone?

I eyed the Mirable Chalice again thoughtfully.

Perhaps there was something I could do. It was risky, but if I wanted to save Barnaby, it was my only choice.

I peered through the veil of underbrush. The campfire smoked sulkily in the faint drizzle. Across the glade, Barnaby stood backed up against the bole of an ancient oak.

"Where is it?" demanded the man with the monocle, pressing the tip of his saber to the boy's throat.

"I don't have it," Barnaby protested. "You're the one with the fancy eyewear, Rencevin. D'you see a stinking magical goblet?"

The man Rencevin snorted. "You've hidden it, then. But I will find it. I always find what I'm looking for, Bagby. Queen Serafine will have her treasure returned. And you will suffer for your crimes, as all thieves must."

"I'm trying to make things right! There's a curse on the Uplands, if you hadn't noticed!"

"You may be able to fool a handful of credulous villagers, but do not expect such tales to work on me, boy. You're no hero. When I'm finished with you, all the world will know what you truly are."

I'd been hoping for the right moment to make my entrance, but as the thief-taker tightened his lips and Barnaby's eyes went wide, I couldn't help myself.

I burst out from the underbrush. "No!"

Rencevin whipped around, drawing a second,

shorter blade as he pressed Barnaby back against the oak with his saber. "Who—? Ah. The bog-witch from Withywatch." He flicked a look at Barnaby. "I suppose I shouldn't be surprised to find you consorting with Bottomland trash." Rencevin's lip curled. He looked at me as if I were a clod of mud stuck to the bottom of his boot. "But she won't be able to help you this time."

"Help him? Why should I help him? Whoever heard of a bog-witch helping someone? Especially him." I jerked my chin at Barnaby. "He's just an overdressed dandy running around doing good deeds, foiling all my evil plans. I'm here for revenge, same as you."

"You are nothing like me, bog-spawn," snapped Rencevin. "I am here to exact the Queen's Justice."

"You'll have to wait, then," I said, drawing myself up even as I ran a cautious hand over my midsection to confirm that the Mirable Chalice was still bound safely beneath my jacket. "Or suffer the wrath of Prunella Bogthistle!" I raised my arms menacingly, wishing I still had that flaming-eye charm.

Rencevin's monocle gave a flash that was no mere reflection. The man grunted, stepping back a pace, though the saber remained at Barnaby's throat. "You have considerable magics, that is true." He continued to eye me cautiously.

Hah! A thread of relief worked free from my bundle

of nerves. The first part of my plan had worked. The magic emanating from the chalice had fooled the thief-taker into believing me a powerful bog-witch. Now I just needed to pull off the rest of the ruse. "Leave the boy to me," I said, "and I just might reconsider turning you into a toad as well."

Rencevin tilted his head. "A nice story, witch girl, but I don't believe you. I think you care for the boy. You've come to help him."

"I have not!" I protested. "I don't care one snit about the boy. Skewer him if you like. I hate him. Stinking heroes."

"Prunella—" began Barnaby, then gasped as the tip of the saber pricked his throat.

I sucked in a gasp of my own, hoping the thief-taker hadn't seen my discomfort. This wasn't working. I needed something more than empty threats. I mustered my strongest glare against them both.

"If I cared about him, would I curse him with the doom of a thousand agonies?" Crooking my finger, I swept my arm out with a flourish, precisely as I'd seen Grandmother do it. I hoped Barnaby would understand.

The boy blinked. Then his eyes narrowed, just for a moment, before he let out a tortured cry.

Rencevin hesitated. "It's not—"

"Would you care to share the same fate, thief-taker?"

I demanded. Barnaby continued to writhe in pre-tended agony. Perhaps a bit too theatrically, to judge by Rencevin's furrowed brow.

"I don't fear you, bog-witch," he said. "Bagby will face my justice."

If only I could truly curse! I stabbed my crooked finger at Rencevin. "Leave. Now. Or by the bones of Esmeralda I *will* curse you!"

Searing light leapt from my finger, sizzling into Rencevin's chest. I shrieked, startled. A hot pain surged through me, arcing from my torso to my hand. I staggered back, eyes watering, distantly aware of the thief-taker cursing and shouting.

Then Barnaby was beside me, seizing my hand, pulling me away. I ran hunched over against the heat that continued to blaze out of the Mirable Chalice. What had I done?

"Are you sure you're all right?" Barnaby asked for the fifth time. "You were yowling like a wet cat."

"I told you, I'm fine," I said. "Not even a mark. All the same, though, I'm glad that thing is on your back." I glanced at the sack slung across Barnaby's shoulders, where the Mirable Chalice rested safely once again. We were walking along a stretch of road that skirted a grassy marshland. The drizzle of rain had finally cleared, leaving the sky changeable and spangled with intermittent shafts of light. "And it wasn't nearly as bad as *your* yowling," I added.

"Hey, I was trying to help. Rencevin didn't believe you." Barnaby chortled. "He'll think twice next time, after that curse."

"I'm not sure it was a curse," I admitted. "That chalice is filthy with magic. It just flared up when I was pretending to curse the thief-taker." I crooked and uncrooked my fingers. Was that what a true curse felt like? A fire ripping through you—an angry, tormented thing?

"Whatever it was, it saved our hides. Well, mine at least. You didn't have to come back for me. I figured you'd be halfway to the Bottomlands before I got out of that scrape, once you saw what was in the sack."

I turned on him, stung. "I wouldn't just leave you there!"

"Hey, don't shout. I didn't know you cared, that's all," he said, looking far too pleased with himself. "Thanks."

"I care about getting my grimoire, and I'd just as soon not see you get skewered. So I suppose . . . you're welcome. Now," I said, to change the subject, "would you like to explain why you were on a quest for the Mirable Chalice when you had it in your pack all along?"

"I'd be happy to, if you'd like to explain why you insisted it was in Lord Blackthorn's manor."

"Grandmother said it was there," I protested. "I mean, she was pretty sure."

Barnaby raised his eyebrows.

"All right, fine," I said. "It was mostly just an excuse."

"To get that grimoire."

My face grew hot. "Yes, well, it's better than me turning you into a frog, isn't it? Anyway, you knew it wasn't there. You're the one who stole the blasted thing, though I don't know how. You must have snitched it right out from under the queen's nose."

Barnaby held his chin a bit higher. A flash of sunlight caught his hazel eyes. "It wasn't that hard."

My breath lodged somewhere in my throat. "You must be the best thief in all the Uplands."

"Well, the queen didn't have any soul-eating crow charms. Just a couple flipping good locks and a passel of enchanted suits of armor. Too slow for me." His smile dropped away, his glib mood passing as quickly as the glow of the sun. "I don't want to be a thief, though, not anymore. Sweet hills, I wish I'd never heard of the Mirable Chalice." He strode ahead, slashing his hand through the grasses that dared nod their heads out over the road.

"Are you angry?" I asked, hurrying to keep up. "I won't call you a thief again if you don't like it."

He didn't look at me, but he slowed his furious pace

slightly. "Trouble is, I *am* a thief. My whole family are thieves." Barnaby produced a silver coin from somewhere about his person. He flipped it back and forth as we continued on.

"He called you Barnaby Bagby," I prompted.

"My da was the first Bagby to take up thieving." Barnaby looked ahead as he spoke, staring at the dark blur of distant trees. "Not because he was a bad sort. He was just hungry, and he had five sons and a wife who were hungry, too. People say Serafine's a good queen, but she wasn't good to us. Or maybe she just didn't know what was going on. Taxes so heavy a fellow had to work day and night to pay 'em. Who's to blame a man for stealing a bag of rice here, or a few copper pennies there, if his family's starving?"

I shook my head. Barnaby forced a sort of strained lightness into his voice, but the rawness underneath trammeled my own heart.

"They caught my da creeping out of the Royal Gardens with a goose. A lousy stinking goose. He begged for mercy, told them it was just to feed his family. And what did he get? Did the fair and lovely Serafine have mercy? She dines on gold and has a gown for every day of the year, so what's one goose to her?"

I had no words. I just walked onward, trying not to flinch at the tautness of Barnaby's shoulders.

"She had him branded for it. 'T,' for 'thief,' right on his cheek. It festered. He died raving in a fever not long after."

We walked in silence for a ways before Barnaby went on. "Mam tried to keep things together for a while, but she wasn't strong. Her body, I mean. She had a fine, fiery spirit. Sort of like . . . Well, anyway, she died, too, and then it was just me and my brothers. I'm the youngest, so they watched after me. It was around then my brother Booth took to thieving.

"Not for geese, though. No. I remember him coming home one morning, before sunup, and tossing gold coins over the rest of us, like a shower of sunshine you could catch in your hand. Wasn't long before the rest of us were at it, too."

Barnaby glanced sideways at me. "You probably don't know what it's like to have folks sneer at you and point. To walk along a street and feel like the lowest grub squashed under someone's fine boot heel. I mean, if they did, you wouldn't care."

He scuffed his boot against the road, kicking aside a clod of dirt. "But I did. So, when those gold coins turned into sausages and cheese and velvet jackets and silk shirts, it was like . . . magic, I guess. It was like one of those charms from the stories that turn the frog into a prince. We were suddenly princes. I'd walk down the street and girls would smile at me behind their frilly fans. I'd go into a tea shop and folks would bow and give me the best table."

"So what changed?" I asked, after he'd been silent several long minutes. "It doesn't sound like a bad life."

"What changed was a locket," he said. "I didn't really need it—Booth had us running bigger schemes than bitty pickpocketing by then. But . . . do you ever do things just because you can? Eat a slice of pie because it's there in front of you? Tell a lie because you know you can get away with it?"

I shrugged, but he wasn't looking at me in any case. "Anyway, the girl I nicked it from started bawling soon as she realized it was gone, raving about her dead mam. Some other folks had to carry her into the tea shop. I should have just gone on my way, sold the blasted thing, and been done with it. She was rich enough to buy another. We never took from poor folks. Even Booth stuck to that."

I wrapped one of my braids around my finger, feeling for bits of my home that were no longer there. "So what did you do?"

"What do you think? I gave it back. Said I'd found it lying in the street." He quickened his pace, as if trying to escape the memory. "She kissed me. Gave me a ruby ring right off her finger. Spouted some long story about the locket being a keepsake from her mam . . . She was so happy, and I just wanted to sink into the pits."

"So you stopped?"

"Booth and the others thought I'd gone soft. Said I'd lost my nerve. Didn't have the guts. I figured I'd show them."

"You went after the queen's treasury," I said.

Barnaby nodded. "Let Serafine bawl over a blasted goblet. I couldn't give a flipping frog, after what she did to my da. And she's got plenty of other trinkets to console her, I can tell you that."

"What did your brothers say when you brought back the Mirable Chalice?"

"I never went back. I didn't have the chalice a day before I was cursing myself for taking it."

"Why? It *is* stinking heavy . . ."

Barnaby snorted. "No. That's when Rencevin caught up with me the first time. He'd been sniffing after us Bagbys for a while, but when the chalice went missing he really put his nose to the ground. I only got away because he hates the Bottomlands more than I do and didn't follow me in. I'll die before I let anyone brand me."

"Why didn't you just say you found the chalice on the street?" I asked.

"That might work with a locket, but it wouldn't fool Rencevin."

"Then just leave it somewhere. Let some scullery maid find it and get the reward."

He tightened his jaw and said nothing.

I sucked in a breath. "You want it. Even after all that. You want the queen's reward. Fame and fortune."

"I told you that when we first met," he retorted. "If I'm the champion of the chalice, none of us Bagbys will ever have to steal again."

"That's why you were in our garden," I said, suddenly understanding. "You were going to say we'd stolen it. We were going to be your scapegoats!"

"It would've made a good story, too," he said. "But then you had to go and save my life and follow me around. And you wanted that blasted grimoire so badly. Anyway, stealing the chalice back from Lord Blackthorn was just as good—even Rencevin couldn't naysay a tale like that."

"What about the curse?" I said. "Pogboggen and the hair charm and all those people wasting away." I fingered the star-shaped buttons of my jacket, remembering Mary Morland's hungry eyes.

"D'you think I'm heartless? 'Course I want to help them. It's my fault they're in this mess. There've been days I nearly walked right into one of these pokey towns and left the chalice on the mayor's doorstep."

"And . . . ?"

"I tried not to think about it. I tried just to pretend I was some grand hero. But it's not true. Folks shouldn't be cheering me. They should be throwing me in irons and tossing me into the pits."

"Now, that's ridiculous," I said. "Everyone knows thieves get their hands chopped off."

"It's not a joke, Prunella," said Barnaby fiercely. "This has gone on long enough. I know what I've got to do."

"You're going to turn yourself in?" I hastened to keep up with his long strides. "After I went to all that trouble saving you from Rencevin?"

"No. But I'm going to turn over the blasted chalice. It was all a lie anyway. I wasn't meant to be a hero. Time to stop pretending."

Chapter 6

I closed my eyes and breathed in deeply, savoring the rich green scent of the swamp. So close to the Night of a Thousand Frights, the air was thick with magic, spicier than the hottest hot-leaf, wild and free. Each breath filled me with vigor and yearning. My grandmother and aunts and second cousins once removed would be busy collecting wood, piling up the bonfire. Ezzie and the other cousins would be hunting fireflies, gathering brilliant clouds to ward against the terror and the power of the coming night. The ache of not being there throbbed through me.

"Hurry up, Prunella!"

I opened my eyes to see the last sliver of the sun across the swamp. Barnaby himself had nearly vanished behind a clump of waygrass. He waited for me at the bend in the boardwalk, where the gray walkway curved out into the wetlands. His eyes flickered restlessly over the sea of grasses surrounding us.

"The village is right up there," I said. "And we haven't seen a sign of that thief-taker for miles. No need to be jumping around like a marsh rabbit."

"Any marsh rabbit worth his ears would be snug in a burrow by now," Barnaby said as we continued. "Considering what's coming tomorrow."

"Pff! If it's the Thousandfold Night that has you all knotted up, stop worrying. I'll keep us safe." I waved my hand airily.

It wasn't *all* bravado. On the Night of a Thousand Frights, the boundary between Uplands and Bottomlands meant little. In the past hour alone, I'd found a handful of rushes that sparkled when I looked at them sideways. Of course, all I knew how to do with mudrushes was to summon globs of mud. Useful for driving off an annoying younger cousin, but probably not much else. Never mind, I told myself. A few foraging trips and I would be fully restocked.

Barnaby remained silent. Despite what he said, I knew what was really bothering him. I could tell by the way he bent under his pack as if it were full of boulders, the way he stared at his boots and crumpled his fine purple cap in one hand.

"Listen, Barnaby, maybe there's another way to deal with the curse," I began.

He wouldn't meet my eyes, staring off over the swamp instead.

"It said something in that book, the one I burned, about knowledge to break the—"

His eyes widened. "What's that?"

I turned, following the line of Barnaby's finger. Something glittered through the swishing grasses.

"The sun on the swamp?" I offered. "Fireflies? Fox fire? Someone out for a last bit of eel-fishing?" I squinted, trying to catch the flicker of reddish light.

"It looks like eyes." Barnaby smothered a yelp. "Flaming eyes."

My stomach squeezed into a knot. It did look like eyes. And a leering mouth. The grasses quivered. Was that a branch? Or a sticklike hand?

"Jacks!" hissed Barnaby. "Run!"

Our footfalls clattered along the boardwalk. I gulped the air. It burned in my chest. I didn't look back. Ahead, the gray walls of Nagog loomed up from the marshland.

The boardwalk ended. I stared in dismay at the village palisades, edged with a thicket of sharpened sticks. I pounded my fists against the gates. They did not move.

"We've got to get inside," panted Barnaby. He

peered along the wall. "Filthy fens! The whole place is walled in."

I threw myself at the gate, but it merely quivered. Barnaby stopped me before I could batter myself again. "Wait." He jumped up lightly, catching hold of a crack between the logs that formed the walls. A moment later, he was pulling himself over the wall and picking his way through the hedge of sharp sticks. Then he was gone. I heard the distant thump of his feet on the far side.

"Hold on," he called. "It's locked and barred. They sure didn't want anything getting in." Wood creaked. Was it behind me?

I tightened my grip on the mudrushes, a desperate laugh catching in my throat. I doubted that globs of mud would halt jacks. But I had to do something, anything, to fight back. I hadn't come this far to end up rent to bits by knobbly wooden fingers. I whirled around to face the swamp.

A slight breeze stirred the dark grasses. The only glimmers were stars sparkling in the eastern sky.

With a click of metal and a grinding of wood, the gates shuddered open. Barnaby bounded out. "Come on! Inside!"

"Barnaby," I said, "look."

He turned, his dagger raised against the darkness.

Slowly, he lowered it. "They're gone. Or they weren't jacks after all."

I frowned, peering more closely at the gates of Nagog. "Lucky for us either way. These gates wouldn't have stopped real jacks for long."

"No wards?"

"Not anymore. Look here, you can see the carvings. They were very good, once." I frowned at the swirling marks running along the fat logs that held up the gate. "But it's just like the charm on the well in Sweetwater. The magic's all faded away."

"So they're defenseless."

I fiddled with the ends of my mudrushes. "Maybe they were sensible and they've already gone away somewhere safe. It's as dead as a tomb in here." I squinted along the empty street. The wide main road was edged with storefronts, but all were shuttered and dark. "We might need to find another village to ditch the chalice in."

"No. I smell smoke."

I sniffed, catching a whiff of cookfires. Straining my ears, I could just make out the murmur of conversation inside one of the buildings. Barnaby drew the Mirable Chalice out of his pack. He stared at it for a long moment, turning it to catch the faint starlight. Then he stalked over to the doorstep of the building where we had heard voices and set it down with a clink.

We retreated behind a shadowy stack of eel traps piled across the way. Barnaby lobbed a palm-sized stone at the door. *Thunk.*

Several moments passed, but the door remained shut and the murmurs continued.

"Come on," said Barnaby, hefting another rock. "Stop chitchatting and come take the blasted chalice. You'll be the hero of the Uplands."

"No worries," I said, directing Barnaby's attention to the gate. "Here comes someone else. Maybe they'll see— Oh no."

The three tall, thin figures advancing from the gloom outside were not villagers. They were not even human. Their bulging heads were too large, their narrow bodies too sticklike.

"Jacks," said Barnaby. He pulled out his dagger. We both pressed ourselves deeper into the shadows.

It didn't matter. The jacks ignored us entirely.

"Where are they going?" Barnaby whispered. "What are they— No!"

With a yell of fury, Barnaby jumped from behind the eel traps. He was as quick as a cat, but the jacks were faster. By the time I joined Barnaby in the street, one of the jacks had seized the Mirable Chalice.

"Give that back!" cried Barnaby.

Another jack turned its misshapen face toward us.

The flames in its eye sockets flared, snapping red and gold. A crackling, papery voice hissed out: *It is his. It has always been his. Do not stand in his way.*

"Who?" I demanded.

Those who work against him will only find misery and woe. Beware the wrath of Lord Blackthorn.

"I'll show you misery and woe!" Barnaby ran at the jack holding the chalice, only to be tackled by the one that had spoken. It laced spindly fingers round his neck.

"Let him go!" I shouted. I threw myself at the jack that had Barnaby and latched both hands around its head, my nails sinking into the spongy pumpkin-flesh. Barnaby's strangled gasps hammered my ears. I yanked with all my strength.

Pop!

I fell. The pumpkin head rolled to the ground with a hollow thud. Barnaby pulled free at last. I scrambled to my feet, backing away from the jack as it careened from side to side, searching for its head.

"The chalice," croaked Barnaby. The jack with the chalice was stalking out the gate even now, leaving the third to guard its retreat.

"Go!" I shouted. "Get the chalice!" I brandished my mudrushes at the guard, driving it back for a moment.

Taking this opening, Barnaby sprinted through the

gate and off into the gloom beyond. I continued to wave my mudrushes menacingly, hoping the jack would be stupid enough to believe I could harm it. If I could just give Barnaby enough time, he might have a chance of getting the chalice back. But against two jacks or, worse, three . . .

A scrabbling sound down the street drew my attention. Esmeralda preserve me. The decapitated jack had located its missing head! Even now it set the gourd back on its spindly neck. The flaring eyes swiveled around to regard me with empty malice.

I held my ground, beginning the mud-splatter incantation. At least I'd go out fighting. With any luck, I'd blind them for a little while.

Before I could finish, they were gone, whisking right past me and out the gate. "Blast it all!" I spun around, preparing to chase after them.

The door to one of the buildings crashed open. Light streamed from within as several figures jostled out into the street, blocking my way to the gate.

Idiot villagers. Why couldn't they have come out earlier, when we needed them? Now I was in the pickle pot, good and stewed.

One of the men snorted like a horse that had found a bee in its hay. "Jacks! Here, in the village? And the gates wide open! Porter, didn't you lock up?"

"I left those gates as tight as the mayor's purse not an

hour ago." The woman named Porter raked me up and down with her stern gaze. She was long and narrow in her wide skirts, a broomstick who looked ready to sweep me away with the rest of the trash on her streets.

"Who are you, missy?" she demanded. "What are you doing, breaking into our village on the night before the spirits walk?"

I could feel my otherness; it was in the way I carried my dress, my hair, even in how I stood and the tightness of my fingers on the mudrushes. They could see it, and their fear prickled my skin.

"I—I'm a traveler," I stammered.

Porter stared at me a long moment, her nose flaring as if she could smell the mud under my fingernails. "No, I can see what you really are, mire-spawn. A bog-witch!" She spoke the words with such loathing it shivered me to my core. "What evil will you set upon us now?" She moved so fast I had time only to yelp. Her iron-hard fingers seized my arm, twisting it sharply. I gasped in pain, and outrage.

"I haven't done anything!" I shouted, thrashing against her grip.

"You'll pay for the evils you've caused us, missy!" Porter loomed over me, more terrifying in that moment than Grandmother had ever been. The rage in her eyes froze my limbs.

She was going to kill me. I held out my handful of mudrushes, stammering the words, the only slim hope I had of breaking away. Then that horrible angry face was gone, slathered in a glob of dark mud. Porter gargled. Her grip on me loosened. I tore myself free, staggering back.

I looked for the gate, but lights flared on all sides, dazzling me. Angry faces shone out from the darkness.

"It's a bog-witch!" shouted someone.

"Stop her!" came another cry.

I ran. A dark, unforgiving shape rose up in my path. Fingers dug into my flesh. I shrieked every curse I could think of, but it was all just words. Something cold and heavy clamped around my wrists. They had shackled me.

"You fools! You'll regret this! I'll—I'll—" I opened my mouth, but I had no more words, and no more mudrushes. What would they do to me now? And where was Barnaby?

I stared at the iron bars of my prison, trying to rally my spirits. Mistress Porter had informed me that I would stand trial upon the morrow, then suggested rather loudly that they'd better start gathering wood for a bonfire. Wonderful. At least I had almost a whole night to get out of this mess.

Of course, that also meant I had a whole night to

worry about Barnaby. Had he recovered the chalice? Or was he lying out in the swamp even now, hurt or . . .

I wished the cell were larger. I couldn't think huddled up in a corner. I needed to pace. Surely then I could think of some charm that would bend iron or break stone and get me out of here. Or perhaps I could turn myself into a crow, as Grandmother did, and escape between the bars of my narrow window.

Oh, what was the use? Here I was with an entire village terrified of me, convinced I was a real bog-witch. Wouldn't Grandmother be pleased? Except that if I were a real bog-witch I'd have escaped already, and cursed the fools with the doom of a hundred misfortunes. I wouldn't have used up all my supplies doing good deeds just because of some boy.

But that wasn't the only reason I'd done them. I remembered the girl who'd given me the pumpkin tart. I had done the right thing, I had chosen my path, and now I was stuck on it. Had I changed? I stared down at my hands, at the bog mud under my nails. I folded them against my chest, hugging myself. I was still me. I was still Prunella Bogthistle.

The outer door creaked. "Barnaby?" I leaned eagerly against the bars, then sagged in disappointment.

"Hello?" A boy of about my own age had entered the building. One hand was wrapped around the collar of a large bloodhound. The other held a tray. I could see the steam rising from it. The boy's cloud of dark hair haloed his face; I couldn't make out his features in the darkness.

The dog padded forward, with the boy following, never dropping his hand from her collar. As he neared the bars, I realized his eyes were looking not at me but off into some middle space. He lifted his hand and felt along the bars until he came to the door. He lowered his tray to the ground, then slid the hand through the gap beneath the door.

The bloodhound looked at me, her face a mass of mournful wrinkles. "Are you going to eat it?" asked the boy.

My stomach growled, so I pulled the tray toward me. It held a wedge of cornbread, some stewed greens, and a bowl of beans. The boy crossed his legs, taking a seat on the floor beyond the bars. The bloodhound sat beside him.

I bit into the cornbread. It was delicious—sweet and buttery. "Do you normally feed your enemies this well?" I asked.

"There's this, too." He fumbled in his pocket and drew out a slightly squashed packet, which he pushed through the bars to me. It held a cranberry turnover. "Sorry if it's smashed. I had to stuff it away so my aunt wouldn't see."

"Your aunt?"

"Helen Porter. I'm Halbert. And this is Cricket." He patted the dog.

"Your aunt's the one I drenched with mud?" I put down the cornbread.

Halbert set his hand on Cricket's neck, smoothing the dog's brown-and-black fur. "I live with her. Sometimes *I* want to drench her in mud. But that's not a good reason to burn someone."

"What if that someone is a wicked bog-witch trying to destroy the Uplands?"

"Is that what you are?"

Although I knew it was impossible, I felt as if the boy were looking right into me at that moment. "No," I said. "I mean, I am a bog-witch. But I'm not trying to hurt anyone."

"I could tell you weren't the one," said Halbert. "When I heard you shouting."

"What do you mean, 'the one'?"

Cricket craned her neck so Halbert could reach a particularly itchy spot. He concentrated all his attention on the dog for a long moment. "You aren't the bog-witch who cursed me to be this way." He gestured toward his eyes. Cricket laid her wrinkled head on his knee. He stroked her long ears absently.

I had already reduced my cornbread to a pile of

crumbs. Now I pulled my hands away before I did the same to the turnover and ended up with blood-red fingers. "A bog-witch made you . . . blind?"

"It was about three months ago. I'd drawn a picture of her," Halbert said. "I was on one of the walkways, looking out into the swamp. I saw her out in a coracle, gathering water lilies. I thought she looked interesting. My father told me I should practice drawing all sorts of things, ugly things, broken things. Not just flowers and fruit and pretty girls. He's a painter, in Orlanna. I was going to go and apprentice with him when I turned thirteen."

"Oh." I chewed my lip. "So I guess she didn't like you drawing her?"

"When she noticed, she practically flew across the water at me. She said how dare I take her likeness and all sorts of horrible things. I tried to say I was sorry, but she didn't listen."

"And you went blind, just like that?"

"After she yelled, she touched my face. Here." Halbert tapped his temple. "I was in a fever by the time I got home. It lasted three days, Aunt Helen said. When it was gone, all I could see was a bit of light and dark. I can still tell when it's noon. That's it."

"Do you know her name?" I asked. "The bog-witch?" My voice shook.

"She didn't say."

"Do you still . . ." The words wouldn't come out. I didn't want to look at the drawing. I didn't want to see my grandmother's face and know it was she who had done this. "An image of someone has a powerful magic," I began. "Another wizard could use it . . ." My words fell away, hushed by the heavy weight on my heart.

"I'm sorry," I said finally. "There's no excuse."

After a moment, I plucked the cranberry pastry up, holding it back through the bars. "Here. I can't . . . I don't care for cranberries much. You have it."

"Are you sure?"

I nodded at first, forgetting. "Yes. Go on. And head back home, before you get in trouble with your auntie. I don't need her any more angry with me than she already is."

"I tried to tell her it wasn't right," the boy said.

"Don't worry," I said. "Thanks for the dinner."

Then he left, padding away with one hand on Cricket's neck. I waited until the door closed behind them. Then I did cry, curse me. Because, for the first time, I didn't want to be a bog-witch. And if I wasn't, what else could I be?

I drew myself upright to confront the host of unfriendly faces glaring at me from every corner of the large saloon. They sat propped on stools and up on the bar, they jammed themselves into the balconied upper level to peer down at me. Every person in Nagog seemed to have crammed into the building.

They had put me near the crackling hearth. I wondered if they had chosen the spot so as to pitch me more easily onto the coals after whatever excuse for an inquisition they managed to put forth.

I would not sniffle. I would not tremble. I would not let them see how terrified I was. I heaved my hands against the weight of the manacles, trying to smooth back my flyaway hair. The first two rows of townspeople jostled back at the motion. It made me feel a little better.

I glanced toward the formidable oaken chair across the floor. The man who sat in it was small, with roving black eyes and the teeth of a rat. Seeing the curl of his lip, I didn't hold much hope that the mayor would be any more forgiving than his people. Mistress Porter had not left my side. Even now she thumped a large staff ominously against the floor, looking as if she wished I were under it.

The hum of conversation dimmed as the mayor stood and raised his hands. "People of Nagog, grave danger has come to our fair village, and we are here to decide how we will deal with it. You see here before you a creature most foul, an evil spawned in the depths of the Bottomlands, that fearsome land of untrammeled magic that birthed the doom of the Uplands so long ago."

The mayor motioned to Mistress Porter. She gave a particularly energetic thump of her staff. "Abel and I found this bog-witch at the town gates last night. She'd used her unspeakable magics to unlock and unbar them, and summoned forth her foul jacks to menace our town. When we confronted her, she revealed her true evil and cast her dark magics on me."

A rumble passed through the crowd. The mayor nodded. My heart squeezed to a lump of coal. I was doomed.

But I wasn't going to go meekly. "Yes, I am a bog-witch," I began. "And that walking hatchet is lucky all she got was a mud-dousing. I didn't summon the jacks! They work for Blackthorn. I was only . . ." I couldn't very well tell them I had wanted to plant the Mirable Chalice on their doorstep. "Oh, you'd never believe me anyway, you ignorant id— Oof!"

Mistress Porter jerked on the chain that ran from my manacles, making me stagger to one side, closer to the fire. "None of your curses, witch! We know your kind!"

"You can't even tell the difference between an insult and a curse," I spat. Shouts and cries broke out all around, not the least of which were Porter's bellows.

"What about the wards?" someone cried.

"Did she destroy them?"

"Will the frights take us all?"

The mayor's voice silenced them. "My friends. I think you will all agree that, of any of us, Mistress Porter knows best the evils of the bog-witches."

Porter spat near my feet. "To my lifelong sorrow."

The mayor went on. "The girl has admitted she is one of the Bottomlander hags, and we have the testimony of several upstanding citizens that she was doing evil to our village. We must take swift action. With the Night of a Thousand Frights upon us and our wards gone, we must ensure the safety of the village."

"This town and everything in it are just so much ghoul feed," I muttered. "And you'd rather sit around calling me names. You ought to be running. Or preparing to fight."

"You see?" Porter said. "She calls for our deaths!"

The mayor tapped his fingers against the solid oak of his chair. "Mistress Porter, it is in your charge to maintain the gates and organize our town watch. What do you suggest?"

Porter fixed me with a cold glare. "I say we use her. Burn her at the gates. Tonight, at dusk. That ought to drive off the darkest demons of the swamp."

"Yes, burn her!" called other voices from the crowd, taking up a chant.

The mayor nodded. "So be it."

The shouts continued. I wondered if their fervor might drive them to the deed then and there. Maybe it would be better to get it over with. I tried to stand upright, to throw my shoulders back, but my whole body trembled. The heat of the nearby hearth seemed to burn my skin, and the whiff of smoke made me gag. I looked up, but the high windows above the balconies were blocked by the rafters. If there had been a crow circling above, I couldn't have seen it. And why should I expect Grandmother to care in any case?

But Barnaby, him I had expected. He must have wondered where I was by now. Had the jacks gotten him? What if he was lying battered and bleeding in mire? What if . . .

What if he was striding into the saloon that moment?

His purple coat gleamed, his smile sparkled, his face glowed with goodwill and enthusiasm. "Greetings, people of Nagog!" He spun around in a slow circle, waving a jaunty greeting to each corner of the room, and contriving to set his long coat swirling rather dramatically. "My name is Barnaby. Perhaps you've heard of me?"

The chanting faltered, then fell away to a silence broken only by one last thump of Porter's staff.

"Weren't them mummers who passed through last week telling tales of a hero named Barnaby going around and fixing the curse of the lost chalice?" said one man.

"Not just fixing the curse," said a young woman, staring at Barnaby. "He's on a quest to find the Mirable Chalice!"

"Yes," Barnaby said grandly, "I have set forth on such a quest. But that's not what has brought me to your fair village. I see you've been having some trouble with this bog-witch?"

All eyes turned to me. I realized I was still standing slack-jawed, and snapped my lips together. Barnaby gave me the barest of winks. It was not reassuring.

"It is true that this girl was once a bog-witch, spawned in the depths of the Bottomlands," he said. "But she is not the danger you think she is. She has been traveling with me these past weeks, and has renounced her evil ways. With my guidance, she has taken up a new calling, and is seeking to help avert the curse upon the Uplands."

Everyone stared at Barnaby, including me.

"She cursed me! She's still a bog-witch," sputtered

Porter. "She ought to pay for what she and her kind have done!"

"And she will," Barnaby replied, dipping his hat to Mistress Porter. "It was the knowledge of the crimes of her kinfolk that first drove her to repent, and it is to atone for these evils that she now seeks to do good works. She has much knowledge of magics; with her aid, the village of Nagog can be protected from the frights that tonight will bring. Free her now, and allow her to prove that she has cast aside her wicked ways."

As he finished this extraordinary speech, Barnaby looked to me, brows lifting in unspoken query. I pursed my lips. The village of Nagog had not done much to inspire me to help them. Then I remembered Halbert. Not to mention the bonfire waiting for me outside. I gave a brief nod.

Barnaby turned to the mayor. "Master Mayor, you have the chance here to ensure the safety of all your village. I can see you are a clear-sighted man. Please consider this opportunity, and have mercy on the bog-wi—the girl, I mean."

The mayor drummed his fingers again. "Well. Hmm. We aren't without mercy here in Nagog. If she really is trying to atone and is willing to swear as much . . ."

"Of course, Master Mayor. If you'd allow me to

talk with Prunella privately, I'm sure that can be arranged."

The mayor sucked on his teeth for a moment, then nodded. Mistress Porter grumbled but yielded to a look from the mayor. She yanked me, none too gently, away from the hearth and into an alcove along the side. Barnaby followed. Porter shoved the chains into Barnaby's hands with a dour look, then stalked away to take up a position between us and the door.

"You came back," I said.

Barnaby glanced around. He spoke in a low voice. "Of course I came back. I'd have been back last night, but that battle-ax with the staff was on patrol."

Despite the manacles on my wrists and the mob calling for my blood, I felt happier than I had all day. "I thought the jacks had killed you."

"Hmph. No spindly old pumpkinhead is doing me in, I promise you that. What a humiliating way to go." He cleared his throat. "But blast it, Prunella, they got the chalice."

"I'm sorry," I said. "But we'll get it back. If we survive tonight, that is."

"So you *will* help them? Even after all this?"

"Someone's got to show them what bog-witches are really like," I said. "Even if they did make me sleep on a slab lumpier than my aunt Flywell's nose."

"If it makes you feel better, *I* spent the night tumbled down in a swampwiggen nest. Ended up with bites all over my . . . Well, I didn't sleep much."

"Maybe a little better." My lips twitched, but it wouldn't do for the contrite bog-witch to start giggling. "And now I suppose I'd better swear I've seen the error of my ways before Porter gets carried away and tosses me into the fireplace."

Chapter 7

Of course, most of the populace of Nagog still hated me even after I swore on my grandmother's soul I would help them survive the Night of a Thousand Frights. But with a horde of dark and nasty creatures descending upon us at dusk, I suppose I was the lesser evil. They agreed to give me a chance.

"They don't hate you," said Barnaby. "They're just scared. And you have to admit that you . . . well . . . you're not . . . ."

"Kind and courteous?"

"I was going to say 'your average village girl.'"

"Curse me if I was," I said. "They'd be completely sunk in the mire then. At least with me they've got someone to toss them a rope." I handed Barnaby a bundle of rags.

"Do you think it'll work?" he asked. He eyed the red-stained bits of cloth dubiously. "Cranberry juice?"

"Of course. I think the seeming spell turned out rather well, considering we're in the Uplands. And ghouls aren't particularly clever. By the time one of them gets close enough to tell this isn't blood, it'll be trapped. If you do your job."

"If there's one thing I know, it's traps," said Barnaby. "All right. I'll take them out there now. You think you can avoid getting burned or locked up while I'm gone?"

I looked toward the cluster of villagers over on the porch of the saloon. Mistress Porter stared at me, her arms crossed, looking as if she could set me on fire with the fury of her gaze.

"I'll try," I said.

Barnaby strode away to meet with a second group of villagers over by the gate, who were laden with shovels, tarps, and armfuls of sharpened sticks.

Squaring my shoulders, I turned and advanced upon Mistress Porter and her crew. They'd gotten a long table set up already, holding everything I'd told them to gather: sticks, glue, paint, salt, and various other supplies. Six of them sat on benches around the table. Halbert perched on the step below, a bound book of parchment and a stick of charcoal in his lap. I frowned. The boy looked oddly washed out, despite his warm red-brown skin and dark thatch of hair. I had the impression that a stiff wind might blow him away, like a mist off the mire. I was glad to see Cricket at his side, bolstering him up with her sturdy brown-and-black shoulder. He smiled as I passed by.

The half-dozen faces that greeted me on the porch were decidedly less friendly. No one moved to make me a place to sit down, so I stood at one end. I dumped the handful of loon feathers I'd gathered that morning onto the table. I hadn't been able to scrounge up much: the feathers, a bundle of waygrass that had already been used for the seeming spells, a tiny smidgen of pyre root, some spiderwebs, and a single crow feather. On the other hand, the border between Uplands and Bottomlands was already blurring. Magic was all around, glinting in the air, settling over the shabby gray buildings and weathered boardwalks of Nagog. I'd even found, in the middle of the muddy street, a fishhook that had already picked up enough magic to be of use. But as much magic as there was, I was still just one bog-witch. I needed to arm the villagers with whatever defenses I could.

"We'll start with the featherweight charms," I said briskly. "First, take one of the sticks and a feather . . ." I scooped up one of each and waited for them to follow. Two of the women whispered behind their hands.

Another tightened her grip on the baby slung across her breast. The old man took a slow pull on his pipe, while the younger fellow beside him kept looking toward the gate and mopping his sweaty brow. Mistress Porter only stared.

"Are you just going to sit there?" I said. "Do you want the frights to come in and murder you all, or worse?"

The woman with the baby shuddered. The sweaty man gulped. Mistress Porter stared.

"Well?" I rattled the rod and the feather. "And stop that whispering before I curse you with serpent tongues," I snapped at the two women. They cowed, clutching each other under my glare.

Mistress Porter stiffened. "Have some backbone, Annabella! And you, Carolina, you ought to be ashamed of yourself. You drove off an alligator last month. Don't snivel and shiver. It's what she wants." She sneered at me.

"What I *want* is to get these charms done so we don't all die strangled by disembodied hands or lured away by will-o'-the-wisps," I said.

"Is that what'll happen?" said the woman with the baby, in a voice that sounded as if it had been blown back and forth across the moor.

"Nah," said the smoking man. "The ghouls'll get us first. Tear our flesh to bits and drink our blood."

"No one is getting their blood drunk," I shouted

over the wails that followed the man's lurid warning. "Look here, I'm not going to say it'll be easy. It'll be a lot more work than sitting here and letting some ward you didn't even create keep all the nasties away. But you've still got a wall, and we've got time to do what it will take to fight back."

I turned to Mistress Porter. "I don't want you to snivel and shiver. I want you to get to work. Because I don't want to get torn to bits by a ghoul any more than you do."

Annabella and Carolina picked up rods and feathers. A moment later, so did the sweating man. Then the rest of them. Finally, Mistress Porter seized a rod, her hands grasping it so tightly I was sure she was imagining it to be my own neck. Fine. I didn't need her to like me. I just needed her to believe me.

It wasn't long before a row of fluffy wands lay proudly atop the table. I set the villagers to work on some simple talismans, painting sigils onto strips of cloth. I would need to add the featherweight charms to the wands myself.

I sat myself down on the step near Halbert. The boy had his book open now. Slowly, he moved the charcoal across the surface. He'd gotten the sigil almost right, though the lines were a bit shaky and the cross-marks were haphazard. It was enough to make me draw a breath of surprise. "That's amazing," I said, "I mean, considering . . ."

"Considering I'm blind?" Halbert smiled wryly. He ran one hand over the book. "Did I really get it right? Or are you just saying that to make me feel better?"

"You obviously don't know me very well if you think I'd say something just to make a person feel better. Honestly, it's good. All you missed was the little curl on the warding eye on the left."

Halbert frowned in concentration, making the correction. I took note of the dozens of pages of his book that were flipped back. "Do you still do a lot of drawing?"

He shrugged. "It's the only thing I ever wanted to do, really. Better to do it poorly than not at all. I thought maybe, if I tried hard, it would start to get easier. But it's not. Lately, especially." He rested a thin hand on the parchment. Cricket gave a faint whine, leaning in to lick the boy's face. Halbert smiled, rumpling her long ears in return.

I stiffened, then squinted at Halbert. With the magic of the Thousandfold Night wafting about, it was hard to discern at first. A slight glimmering gust came with each of the boy's breaths. Just as I'd seen when I looked at Mary Morland. *No!*

Something dark and fearful clutched at my insides. Was that Halbert's fate as well? To fade slowly until he lay still and chill and hopeless? I would not let that happen. Halbert had helped me when no one else would, despite what had happened to him. If there was something I could do to make this right, I must do it. But for that, I needed to know the truth.

"Do you . . . did you . . ." I took a breath and forced the question out. "I don't suppose you still have that picture of the witch who cursed you? Or did she take it?"

"She took one of them," he said. "But my father says you should draw something three times to understand it. Here's one of the others." He flipped to the very front of the book.

I leaned away. My heartbeat pounded in my ears. I didn't want to look. But at least I had the option of choosing what I saw. Halbert had lost that. I took a deep breath and turned to peer at the image.

It wasn't Grandmother. It wasn't Aunt Flywell, either, or any of my other relations. I frowned at the figure crouched in a coracle, reaching out to pluck a water lily. She had a prodigious nose and masses of pale hair. "It's brilliant work," I said. "The eyes, especially." They stared up out of the paper, boring into my heart and withering all my courage away.

I squinted. "What's that around her neck? It looks like a bird."

"A peacock, I think. I could only see the necklace when it caught in the sunlight."

"Hmm." I sat back. "She's not a Bogthistle. Unless she's under some sort of seeming spell, but if so, why look like a different bog-witch? I wonder . . . would you let me have it?"

Halbert shrugged. "I can't see it anyway." He carefully tore the page from his book and held it out.

"Thank you." I furled it up and tucked it into the pocket of my coat.

Halbert let the pages riffle back, returning to the page with the sigil. "So," he said, tapping the mark, "will this be any use? I want to help."

"Make as many as you can. We need them."

And ten times more, I added silently. Featherweight charms and shielding sigils were all well and good; they'd keep off the disembodied hands at least. But what about the ghouls? The wights? Esmeralda preserve us if we encountered a spectral stallion. All I could do was to keep working. Soon enough, night would be upon us, and it would be time to fight.

By the time the sun had sunk to touch the western horizon, we had a goodly arsenal of charms, talismans, and shielding. Barnaby found me in the village square, handing out the feathery wands and dividing up the talismans. "Is that all of them?"

I nodded, handing Halbert his papers with their sigils, now charmed with shieldings. He tucked all but one into his pockets. The last he affixed to Cricket's collar.

Barnaby handed me a mug of hot-leaf. It was tepid at best, but I drank it down gratefully.

"So," I asked, around a mouthful of the corncakes he'd offered with the tea, "do you think we're ready?"

"We dug a dozen good pits and set them up with those bloody rags of yours. With any luck, that'll keep the ghouls busy. If we can just keep everything else on the other side of the walls, we should make it through."

I could hear the doubt in his voice. He tried to cover it with one of his rakish grins. "How can we fail? The greatest thief in the lands, and the mightiest bog-witch of them all."

"Hardly. Me, I mean. But I did . . ." I searched through the remaining charms and talismans I'd kept for myself. "Here."

Barnaby stared at the medallion I held out.

"I know it's not much to look at. Just be glad I didn't still have the chicken foot. And it won't do much against anything that's actually alive," I warned as he settled the cord around his neck. "But it should stop the spirits from ripping your soul to shreds."

"Well, that's something." He looked down at the medallion for a moment, then back at me. "Don't you have one for yourself?"

I shrugged. "Only one crow feather. No—you keep it." I held up my hands, forcing lightness and confidence into my voice. "I'm used to dealing with the dark and horrible, remember? It'll do more good for a dandy from the city. You've probably never even seen a bog-wight."

We both jumped as a call rose from the lookouts on the southern wall. It was time.

"I'd better get up there before they start tossing our precious talismans at shadows and fog."

Barnaby nodded. He would remain on the ground, along with the crowd of well-armed villagers prepared to deal with any material threat that made its way over, or under, the walls.

"Prunella," he called, stopping me partway across the square. "Just . . . keep safe. If anything happened to you . . ."

"I'll be fine," I said, holding up my armful of charms. "Bog-witch, remember?" I took a deep breath to drive the tremor from my voice. "Thank you, Barnaby. And don't get yourself killed, either. You'll give me a bad reputation."

Another shout rang out, followed by a sound no living lips had made. The moaning wail turned my blood to ice and nearly froze my feet in place. Then there was no more time. I ran, air burning in my chest, legs on fire, racing to reach the walls.

I clambered onto the scaffolding between Carolina and the pipe-smoking man. The old man shook his feathered wand challengingly and glowered down beyond the wall. As I reached the top, something pale and spiderlike scrabbled up over the hedge of spikes. It tensed, prepared to leap straight at me.

A fluffy wand struck it right in the palm as it leapt, sending the disembodied hand careening away into the night sky. The old man whooped.

"Good work, Elb," cried Carolina. "You show them we're not going easy!"

"So. They really work," said Mistress Porter, from farther along the wall.

I sniffed. She needn't look as if she wished they hadn't. But this was no time for pique. The mist reached out, swarming up from the swamp, stretching to encircle the village with clammy tendrils. More spidery white hands were skittering up the walls. The few that got past the line of wands were dealt with easily by Barnaby and the others below. One did get a grip on the mayor's neck, but Barnaby pried it loose before it could do any serious damage.

"We're doing pretty well!" crowed Elb, puffing out a ring of smoke and punching his wand at the sky.

I only hoped we could keep it up. Between roils of mist, I caught glimpses of lumbering forms with softly gleaming eyes. Wails and moans echoed from the darkness in all directions now. It sounded horribly as if the ghouls were inside the walls with us. Then I grinned, hearing a different sound. A bellow of pain and anger. One of the traps had worked. We might just have a chance.

My hope winked out as a scream plunged deep into my mind, driving away all thought, all faith, all life. I clenched my chattering teeth to keep from biting my own tongue. I was dimly aware of Carolina and Elb bowed down along the wall, panting and moaning. Elb's pipe fell from his lips, casting a shower of embers across the dirt below.

I clawed my way up to peer out over the swamp. Something great and terrible moved there, slipping forward from the mist, closer and closer.

It looked like a horse, but pale, as if lit from within. White bones gleamed beneath the luminous green phantom-flesh. The creature tossed a mane of smoke and ash. Its slitted eyes glinted green in the sockets of its skull.

"Spectral stallion," I said, gripping two spikes in my fists, reminding myself that the world was solid and real. I pulled Elb upright. "Come on, we've got to get ready!"

The creature pawed the ground. Verdant flames shot up from each hoof strike.

"Up! Up!" I shouted. "The talismans! Use the talismans!"

Then it was thundering forward, and I didn't care about the ghouls in the darkness or the spidery hands lurking in shadows. All I could see were those terrible eyes racing toward me. I clutched for one of my own charms. "Now!" I shouted.

A hail of ragged talismans fell across the path of the phantom horse. It reared, snorting. Blasts of green fire shot into the sky. Then it turned aside, disappearing into the mists. I let myself fall against the wall for a moment. That was close. And it wasn't over.

Screams and yelps pulled me out of my momentary stupor. Something was happening farther down the wall. A lithe figure hissed at Mistress Porter from its perch among the hedge of spikes. She jabbed at it with her wand. It moved as quick as a cat, crouching down, slinking along the wall, away from her. The wight blinked its pale eyes, focusing on old Elb, pulling back thin lips to reveal a ridge of sharp teeth. It tensed. Elb swung his wand around as it leapt.

The creature twisted away, falling past the old man. I didn't have time to see where it went, because suddenly Elb was floating several feet above the walls.

"Help!" he called, reaching for Carolina's outstretched hand. His fingers clawed the air, inches away from hers.

Curse it! In a moment he'd drift out over the swamp. I dived for his fallen wand, caught in the spikes along the wall. I brought it down over my knee, snapping it. At once, the man flopped down into Carolina's arms.

Several white spidery things fell as well, slamming into the ground. Barnaby and the others made short work of the hands, which stumbled around drunkenly.

Then it happened. A thunderous crash split the night. The world listed to one side. I scrabbled to grab something, anything, to stay upright. Every other noise was lost in the terrible tumult of the collapsing wall.

I fell. Darkness rushed at me. I slammed into the ground, and pain shot through my arm, my side. I forced myself up, pushing aside a litter of wood and bits of scaffolding. I turned back toward the wall.

Advancing through the great gaping hole came the spectral stallion. Green embers fell from its flaring nostrils as it raised its head. It opened that long snout, licking the air with a serpentine tongue of flame as it paced slowly into the village. The fall of each hoof tolled like a death bell. Moans of terror rose from the scattered clumps of villagers. We were lost.

"Hey, you! Horseface!"

"Barnaby," I croaked. He swaggered forward all alone to face down the creature.

"Why don't you try to feast on my soul?" He danced

to one side as the horse snorted a gust of flames at him. "It's a tasty one, if I do say so myself."

The stallion turned its massive head, leveling its eyes at Barnaby.

"Barnaby!" I struggled to get up.

He flashed me a grin, then turned back to the horse. "Come on, you old nag. Are you scared?"

The spectral stallion screamed. I bowed under the fury of it, struggling to keep my eyes on Barnaby. As the creature hurled itself forward, Barnaby dashed away. The next moment, they were both gone, out into the swamp. Another horrible cry sliced across me.

I ran toward the gap. Mistress Porter met me there, a talisman in each hand and a look of fury on her face. But for the first time, it wasn't directed at me.

"That boy's going to get himself killed," she said. "What does he think he's doing?"

"Saving the rest of us," I said. "Or being stupid. But probably the first." I started out into the swamp. Mistress Porter followed.

"Aunt Helen!" called Halbert, somewhere behind us.

"You stay back," she said. "Keep Cricket close and stay safe. The bog-witch and I have to . . . What's that?"

I followed the line of her finger to a distant flicker of light. Instantly I shut my eyes. "Don't look at it!"

"Look at how it sways, like a dancer. A lovely golden dancer . . ."

"It's not lovely! It's a will-o'-the-wisp, and it's trying to get you out into the swamp, where it can feast on your spirit!" Keeping my eyes tightly shut, I reached for her. I could hear her steps ahead of me. Curse it, the thing had gotten her!

I felt my way forward. Mistress Porter was moving more quickly now. Noises spun around me. The night was a chaos of screams and shouts and moans. The cry of the spectral stallion echoed across the swamp. Where was Barnaby?

I forced myself to concentrate on what was in front of me, whether I could see it or not.

"Prunella?"

"H-Halbert?" I stammered as a hand caught mine.

"Don't worry, I've got you. Go on, Cricket, find Aunt Helen."

I followed as the boy pulled me forward. A few moments later, I collided with Mistress Porter.

"Lovely golden dancer," she murmured.

I seized her. "Snap out of it!" I tried to pull her around, away from the wisp, but she fought back. My handful of charms went flying. I heard them patter onto the spongy ground.

"All right, then," I said, panting. "But you'd better

not throw me in that prison again. This really is for your own good." I slapped her.

She grunted. This time I managed to turn her around, with Halbert helping. "I know it looks beautiful, but it's going to kill you, and, if you're not careful, Halbert, too."

"Halbert?" she said, shakily, in a normal voice.

"Just keep your eyes closed," I said. "Halbert, can you get us back?"

"Cricket can," he said. "Cricket, let's go home, girl."

A low hiss curdled the air. I suddenly became aware that I had no charms, no talismans, nothing but Mistress Porter's hand in mine.

"Porter. Give me your talisman."

"I don't have any. I must have dropped it when— when— Sweet hills, it's a wight, isn't it?"

The hiss sounded again, closer, followed by a clicking sound, like sharp teeth gnashing together. I wanted desperately to open my eyes, but if I was caught by the wisp I wouldn't be able to help anyone.

"Halbert," I said, trying to remain calm, "do you still have your papers? With the sigils?"

"No, I gave them all to the mayor to use against the horse. Wait, there's still . . . Cricket, here, girl."

The rustle of paper set my heart beating again. Crinkled parchment met my fingers as Halbert pressed the page into my hand.

Grasses swished to my left, as if something was passing through them. This was it. I hoped I was facing away from the wisp. I opened my eyes.

No sparkle of mesmerizing light caught me. What I saw instead was worse. The wight stood not three paces away, teeth bared, eyes glowing softly. It lifted its pale, withered nose, nostrils flaring. Then it leaned back, crossing its arms, and let out a long, slithering chuckle.

Cricket growled in return, straining against Halbert's hold to snap at the creature.

"A pup and his pup, and a crunchy old woman. Tasty treats for the Night of Frights, hrmmm . . ." The wight spoke in a voice full of serpents. "But what's this? A bog-witch?" He stepped forward, the movements smooth yet off-kilter somehow, a part of some other world. It turned my stomach. "You ought to be with us, witchling."

"If you know I'm a bog-witch, then you ought to know better than to trifle with me," I said, raising my chin. "This village is under my protection." I turned, calling over my shoulder. "Cricket, home! Go on."

"But—" began Porter.

"Just go! I've got all I need."

They went. The wight slid forward another step. I stepped to match him, blocking his way. The sound of retreating footsteps heartened me. At least Halbert and the others were safely away.

The wight leered. His pale skin stretched tight over sharp bones. "Magic in your veins, yes. But no bog-witch walks with the Uplanders like she's one of them."

"You come one claw closer and you'll find out just how much of a bog-witch I am." I smoothed out the paper in my sweaty fingers. I was going to need something better than a simple talisman for this. A warding sigil wasn't going to do more than slow the wight down. I still had my smidge of pyre root, but without charcoal I—

I *did* have charcoal. Halbert's charcoal sigil.

"You think you can be a lamb, join the flock of Upland sheep with their two-faced shepherdess?" said the wight. "You have the lowland waters in your blood, I can smell it. Come, and we'll crush their paltry wall and feast on their flesh and spirit." He beckoned with a claw-tipped finger. "It is our right, after all they have taken, and all they seek to take."

"I think I'd rather stick to hot-leaf and corncakes," I said, fumbling behind my back with the parchment and my last bit of pyre root.

I hurled the crumpled ball of paper toward him as he lunged, and threw myself to the ground. Fire blossomed in the darkness, consuming the leaping wight.

His shriek was so loud I feared it might crack my bones. I rolled to my feet. The wight crouched, enveloped in flames. He writhed, shaking off the cloud of fire. I hadn't expected my charm to destroy him, but with luck it would drive him away.

"I was wrong." He spat, falling back. "No bog-witch I've known would take the side of the Uplanders."

"Maybe I'm a different sort of bog-witch," I snapped. "Now go. I told you. This village is under my protection."

He snarled, backing away. "They will never love you, witchling. You will regret this one day. She has taken all she can of the green hills and the sheep who tend them, and now she turns her eye to our demesne. There will never be peace between Uplands and Bottomlands." Then he was gone, slithering off into the darkness, leaving only the ghost of his last words: *You will join us, one day.*

I stood for what seemed like hours, watching the shadows where the wight had disappeared. Who was he talking about? Did it have something to do with the curse that had drained the wards and other enchantments?

I started. Someone or something was glopping through the mud toward me.

"Prunella?"

"Barnaby!" My legs suddenly felt as if they might

not support me. But I wasn't imagining it. There he was, whole in body and spirit, striding out of the mists. I ran to meet him. "You—you're alive." I batted him in the arm. "What did you think you were doing, getting that thing to chase you? It could have killed you, or worse!"

"Not me," he said. "Aside from the fact that I'm dashing quick and can outfox a lumbering nag like that even on a bad day, there was also this fine piece of bog-witchery." He tapped the medallion hanging from his neck. He lowered his voice. "Truth be told, even quick as I am, I'd have been shredded to bits if it weren't for your charm. Saved my life, and my soul, too, I'd wager. Thanks." He smiled at me.

"Even a bog-witch likes to keep her friends in one piece," I said.

"So that's what I am?" he said. "A friend?"

I coughed. "Well, yes. Just don't expect me to toss flowers at you."

He grinned. "Never."

Chapter 8

Things went much more smoothly after that. Halbert and Cricket had to drag back a few other unlucky souls who were caught by the wisps, and the disembodied hands never did give up trying to scuttle in and choke the unwary. But with the stallion sunk into the mire and the wight driven off, the night was ours.

"Dawn!" shouted Elb from his lookout on the eastern wall. "I see the sun!"

A rousing cheer went up from the villagers of Nagog. I was too tired to do more than sigh in relief. I leaned against the side of the saloon, then slumped down to sit on the edge of the watering trough. All I wanted was to sleep for a week.

"People of Nagog!" cried the mayor. "Friends, neighbors, and all! We have weathered this storm and persevered in adversity. It was a dark and terrible night, but you have all demonstrated courage beyond measure. Let us celebrate our victory! And let us not forget to whom we owe this victory!"

I scrambled to my feet. Barnaby was standing near the mayor, and I could see him searching for me. Hastily, I ducked back behind a rain barrel. In the gray morning, the shadows would still hide me.

"Barnaby the Brave!" shouted the mayor, seizing Barnaby's arm and flinging it up into the air. A crash of cheering and clapping broke out, punctuated by whistles and whooping.

"It was this lad who, with no thought for his own life, dared to lead the spectral stallion away from our fair village and lured it into the mire. We owe him our lives! Three cheers for Barnaby!"

As the hip-hip-hoorays echoed through the village, I sank down lower behind my rain barrel. It didn't matter. I didn't want cheers. That was why I was hiding like a spider in a dusty corner. I didn't *need* cheers. I had done this because . . . because . . . Oh, blast it! My chest rang hollow with each hooray.

"Wait!" called Barnaby, silencing the cheers. "It's not that I'm ungrateful, folks. I'm glad for your cheers and all. And happy to have been able to do what I could to help. But I'm not your hero today. Or, at least, I'm not the only one."

There was a pause, filled with muttering. I sat still, like a pool on a windless day.

Barnaby went on. "Prunella Bogthistle is the one who saved this village, even though you lot were set to burn her. It's thanks to her we had the magics to drive off those frights. Without her, we'd all have been just so much horse feed."

"He's right."

I stiffened. It was Mistress Porter.

"She may be a bog-witch, but she saved me and mine. Though I've got no reason to love the hags from the bog, I know enough to judge a person by what they do, not who their mam is. So I say, three cheers for Prunella, witch of the bog!"

The first cheer was ragged and stuttery. The second trembled the water in the rain barrel. The third pulled me to my unsteady feet.

When I looked out over the square, I saw Barnaby, still searching. Then his eyes met mine. He pushed his way past the mayor to pull me out from the shadows.

This time, all three cheers thundered like the words of some great spell, terrifying and exhilarating. Barnaby took my hand and lifted it up, punching the sky and whooping. I laughed. It was nothing I'd ever expected. Nothing I'd ever sought. But now that I was here, this was where I wanted to be, the most perfect moment in the world.

Barnaby drew me away from the celebrations while the long tables were being cleared of the savory roasts and bean stews to make room for the army of cakes and pies produced in the ovens of Nagog that day. The entire village had slept the morning away, to rise at noon and begin preparations for the victory feast. I was rested, and stuffed, and blissfully content.

Barnaby, on the other hand, looked as if he'd found a pickle in his maple bun. "What is it?" I asked. "Aren't you enjoying yourself? Look at me, with this silly smile slapped on for the past three hours, and I'm a bog-witch. You ought to be dancing on the clouds with all this hullabaloo over Barnaby the Brave, hero of Nagog. Or didn't enough pretty girls give you flowers?"

Barnaby shook his head, his lips stiffening to an unhappy line. "We did good. It's not that I don't care for roasts and cheers and all that. But—phaagh!" He ran his fingers through his hair as he groaned. "Bad enough I stole the chalice in the first place. Now I've gone and lost it."

"Well, that's easily sorted. You've just got to get it back," I told Barnaby. "You're the one who wanted to be a hero. Look at it this way: At least you'll have earned it now. No need to gloom around feeling guilty like you've been doing."

Barnaby gave a muffled groan. His head had been sunk into his arms since we sat down at the table in the saloon. He didn't even touch the cranberry pie I'd brought him from the feast table.

"This is supposed to be a victory party, you know," I said. "You might try to buck up for the sake of the villagers. Like I said, at least this way you can really get it back. That ought to satisfy that Rencevin fellow. And the book said something about the knowledge to break the curse being in the Mistveil. Besides, I need my grimoire."

"You still want that thing?" Barnaby asked. "I thought, after all this . . ."

"What, that I'd settle down and run a tea shop? Hardly. I mean, the cheering and feasting aren't bad," I said, trying to sound careless. "But it's not the same as . . ."

"As what?"

I wasn't about to tell Barnaby that all I wanted was my grandmother to smile at me. He'd think it was ridiculous. "Nothing. It's fine. If you're not going to eat, we might as well leave now."

Barnaby set his hands on the table. "You're right.

The sooner we leave, the sooner I get that chalice back and end this stinking curse."

"You can do it, Barnaby," I said, more softly. "I wouldn't have tried to trick you in the first place if I wasn't sure you could get into Blackthorn Manor and get me that grimoire. Bog-witches aren't easily fooled by frippery and bluster. You *are* the best thief in the lands, and you've got the heart of a hero."

"Oh?" He grinned. "Are bog-witches normally good judges of that?"

"Well, you know, I'm starting to think I'm not a normal bog-witch."

"I could have told you that the moment I met you. Come on, let's get going."

It took us four more days to reach the Sangue River, heart of the Uplands, half of which we spent in a fruitless detour out into the wilder borderlands in pursuit of the jacks. Tired and bramble-scratched, we eventually made our way back to the highway.

Barnaby looked longingly toward the curving road. We had halted at the point where it turned to follow the lazy bends of the river north. "If we went that way, we'd be in Orlanna in a week. Quicker if we caught a ride on one of those paddlers." He gestured ahead to Veil's Edge.

Our map called it a "village." "Way station" or "outpost" seemed more fitting to me. The lush woods ran down almost to the water's edge, shadowing a single line of stores and stables. The river, on the other hand, was crowded with boats of all kinds. The largest of the paddleboats rose three levels up from the water: a wide, flat, boxy thing wrapped in white balconies, weighted down in the back by the enormous red-painted wheels.

"We'll be headed north soon enough," I said. "We can take one on the way back. Once we get the chalice."

"You're assuming we won't get stuck in the blackest pits of the Bottomlands," Barnaby said, eyeing the fringes of the bayou on the far side of the river.

"Piffle," I said, waving my hands airily. "We've got the map, so we'll be sure to avoid the worst of it. Besides, it doesn't look *that* bad. Rather pretty, I'd say."

"You're joking, right?" He gestured across the water. "Are we looking at the same thing? That sticky, swampy mess?"

I studied the distant bayou. Pale moss veiled the knobbly trees, like tattered lace wrapped around the shoulders of wise old women full of tricksy secrets. Hidden pools glinted beyond the bent knees of the cypress roots, promising mystery. I shrugged. "We'll be fine. Though I'm not sure your wardrobe will make it through unscathed." I eyed his purple coat and cap. "The Bottomlands are, without a doubt, muddy."

"Well, I suppose a hero has to face his greatest fear one day, right?"

"We'll get a raft," I offered. "That ought to help. Before you know it, you'll be on the way to Orlanna."

"Just in time for the Festival of Masks," Barnaby added as we continued toward the village proper. "Now, *that's* a spectacle. Every single soul in the whole city out on the streets, feasting and singing, wearing the most fantastical masks you've ever seen."

"I don't know. It'd be hard to beat that one over there." I jerked my chin at the waterfront we were approaching. A man stood at the far end of the dock, his face obscured by an elaborate silvery mask curved like the crescent moon. A shimmer of stars seemed to float around his shoulders—sequins or glitter, perhaps.

He was speaking, but we were not yet close enough to make out the words. Whatever it was, it caused a ripple of motion through the dozens of folk gathered around him. The man gave an extravagant sweep of his arm up toward the paddleboat moored behind him. The prow bore the legend *Brilliante*, and she certainly lived up to the name.

From her paddles to her prow, the boat was painted

and scrolled with color. Her shallow hull and single deck were rich orange-gold, set off by green railings and purple trim. The paddles at her stern were black, but even this somber touch was alleviated by substantial embellishments of gold.

Though she was among the smaller vessels docked at Veil's Edge, the *Brilliante* rose out of the water as large as a good-sized cottage. Inscribed flamboyantly upon the cabin wall were the words "Gullet Waterborne Players."

As we drew closer, a voice echoed from the prow. "Frightful and fearsome witch, you shall not find what you seek! For I am Serafine the Valiant, the Adamant, and your wicked powers cannot avail you here!"

A crown rose above the glittering golden mask of the speaker. A fringe of peacock feathers decorated her white robes. "Your dark lord is gone, vanquished by my might and the goodness of the Uplands. Begone, back to the foul pits that bore you." She flung out her hand in a sweeping gesture of warding.

I flinched, but she wasn't pointing at me. A cackle boiled up from the shadows beside the great paddlewheel at the stern of the boat. Skulking forward came a bent, ragged form. All I could see beneath the cowl of her cloak was an enormous green nose, decorated by at least five hairy warts. She raised one crooked finger, uncowed by her queenly adversary. "Fair queen, you do not know the horror that you face. Doom lies upon you if you do not give up the Mirable Chalice!"

Barnaby leaned toward me. "They're doing the Epic of Queen Serafine the First. So that must be Esmeralda, your great-great-great-granny. You reckon they got the likeness?" He smirked. "You don't much look like her, thank the sweet hills."

I would have rolled my eyes, but I was too busy squinting at the witch's mask. There was something about it . . . the Serafine mask, too. The figures shimmered, as if I were seeing them through the air above a fire. Serafine seemed to shine with an inner light, although the high canopy of trees cast the riverbank in shade. And Esmeralda wasn't just some caricature of an old crone. Her crackling voice ran bony fingers along my nerves, stronger than simple mummery.

It was a seeming spell, I'd have sworn it on Grandmother's warts. Just then, a squawking call drew my attention upward. Three crows perched in the branches overhead, peering down at the mummers below. The moon-faced man slipped a glance at his raucous onlookers before continuing. The witch and the queen froze in dramatic poses as he picked up the tale.

"And so fair Serafine the Adamant refused the witch, for the power of the Mirable Chalice was needed to preserve the Uplands in all their glory and to keep their people safe. But Esmeralda was not the only one who sought the chalice . . ."

Two new figures stepped forth. The taller stood enfolded in a voluminous cloak. The other had the pumpkin head of a jack. Its eyes snapped with flames.

The crowd jostled back in alarm. Barnaby let out a whistle of disbelief. "He looks just like a real jack."

I crossed my arms. "It's some sort of enchantment on the masks. They must be very old." I squinted. Just for a moment, the jack had dwindled to a small, plump figure in overlarge robes and a rather silly-looking orange mask. I blinked, trying to steady my vision. The jack stood as spindly and menacing as ever.

"Did you see . . . ?" began Barnaby.

"Yes. I think the charm's fading, just like everything else here." I tapped my fingers together. It still didn't make sense to me. What sort of curse was this?

The cloaked figure spoke then, in a rustling voice that sent shivers down my spine. "I will have my chalice back. Stand against us and you will perish, bright queen. Your magics cannot avail you against the might of Blackthorn." He raised his head to reveal a leathery face like that of a scarecrow, brown and lumpish, yet with deep, dark eyes. The crows above let off another round of croaking.

The performance went on, with Blackthorn convincing Esmeralda to join with him and attack the queen in a last attempt to steal the chalice. The crowd cheered as Serafine thwarted them. Several enthusiastic children from the crowd even joined in, playing the role of the mob of Uplanders who chased the villains off into the Bottomlands.

The moon-faced man capped off the final narration to a rousing round of huzzahs. "Thank you, good folk! We hope to have entertained you with our presentation of the Epic of Serafine. But remember this: All stories have more than one side. If you will grace us with your patronage tomorrow night, we will endeavor to thrill and amaze you once again. More danger! More drama! More magic and wonder! Don't miss your last chance to see the Gullet Waterborne Players before we leave for Orlanna and the Festival of Masks!"

All the mummers had returned to the stage to take their bows. I stared at the masked queen in her feather-fringed white gown. Something was niggling at the back of my brain: a half-formed thought that I couldn't quite grasp.

I didn't realize how lost in the mummery I'd become until Barnaby stiffened in alarm. "Rencevin!"

We ducked behind a broad-shouldered woman carrying a vast bowl of hot-leaf tea. Through the drifting haze of sweet steam, I could just see the gray coat and wide-brimmed hat of the thief-taker on the far side of the crowd.

"This way," Barnaby whispered. "There's a raft over there. If we can just get out on the water without him seeing—"

"Barnaby Bagby!" rang the voice of Rencevin, cutting through the excited chatter of the audience.

"Filthy fens," Barnaby swore as a burly man in a leather jerkin blocked our route across the dock to the raft. Spinning around, we found two more men in leather standing between us and the road. There was nowhere to run. I eyed the river, wondering how many alligators might be lurking.

A murmur rippled through the crowd as they drew aside, forming a path for the thief-taker. The moon-faced man stood with the masked Esmeralda on the prow of the *Brilliante*, watching the scene with the rest.

"Where is it, Bagby?" demanded Rencevin. "Where is the Mirable Chalice?" His golden monocle glinted, flashing a brief gleam of light that did not come from the sun.

"I don't have it," said Barnaby. "Lord Blackthorn has it. And I'm going to get it back from him."

Rencevin strode another pace forward, drawing his saber. "Pretty story, Bagby. But I know the truth."

I was speaking before I even knew my lips were moving. "This is Barnaby the Brave. He's going to go out there into the Bottomlands you all are so terrified of, to face Lord Blackthorn himself and get that chalice back."

Some of the onlookers turned to one another, murmuring. They didn't look convinced, but they didn't look ready to toss us to the alligators, either. The moon-faced mummer bent his crescent head to the hag beside him.

I glared at Rencevin. "If you want your stinking chalice back, don't pester him. He's going to have difficulties enough. Unless you'd rather go get it yourself?"

He flinched. My spirits rose. But he did not retreat.

"Oh yes," Rencevin said. "And tell me, ragtag little girl, why should any of us good and noble Uplanders believe anything you say? Or will you burn them, too, if they do not do as you wish?" He tilted up the brim of his hat, revealing a red weal running from ear to neck.

Curse me, I was the one who flinched then.

Rencevin addressed the crowd. "She's a bog-witch. Do you hear me? And we all know about bog-witches and their wicked ways." He jabbed a finger toward the mummers. "Even these tawdry theatrics tell us that."

"There are many stories in the world," interjected the man in the moon mask. "And we must judge the truth of them ourselves. I, for one, have heard stories drifting from the east, on the lips of travelers. They tell of Barnaby the Brave, the Curse-Killer, Defender of the Uplands."

"You see?" I said, triumphantly.

"I also know, as a player upon the stage, that the masks we wear do not speak to the truth in our hearts. Beneath them can be quite a different person." As he spoke, the man pulled back the silver crescent moon to reveal a thin, malleable face and flyaway hair. The flourish of theatricality drew every eye to the deck of the *Brilliante*.

Under cover of the rising chatter, Barnaby leaned toward me. "Look. The raft."

I gave a huff of surprise. Somehow the craft had pulled free of its moorings and was drifting along the edge of the docks toward us. The burly man hadn't noticed yet.

Then I saw the girl crouched beside one of the pilings farther on, still clad in the white robes of the queen, but without her glittering mask. She beckoned. "The mummers. They're helping us," I whispered. "Why?"

"We can ask later," he said. "You ready to run for it?"

Back on the *Brilliante*, the narrator threw his voice out over the crowd like the rays of the sun, warming and soothing. "We respect the lawful servants of our great and noble Queen Serafine." I frowned, catching an odd note in his speech. Was it sarcasm?

The narrator went on. "Surely there is some misunderstanding here?"

"The misunderstanding is that these two can mean anything but ill toward the people of the Uplands," spat Rencevin. "Barnaby Bagby stole the Mirable Chalice, and he will pay for it."

"Now, now," said the mummer, raising his hands. "Can't we solve this peacefully?"

An explosion of light and smoke burst from somewhere near the *Brilliante*'s great paddles. Screams rose from the crowd. Suddenly everyone was moving.

"Get to the raft, Prunella!" called Barnaby. The burly man gave a roar and charged toward us. Barnaby flung himself into the fellow, sending them both to the ground. He rolled free, regaining his feet as the other man groaned and lifted his head.

I jumped from the dock onto the raft. Taking up the pole, I prepared to push us off, out into the faster currents. When I turned to look for Barnaby, however, my heart sank into my boots. He was running for the raft quick as a hare, but a hound was on his trail.

Rencevin bared his teeth. He held his saber raised, ready to slash at Barnaby's back.

Then, suddenly, the thief-taker, too, was sprawled

out across the dock, his golden monocle flying free on its thin chain. I caught just a glimpse of a small, pumpkin-headed form ducking away into the crowd.

There was no time to learn more. Barnaby launched himself through the air toward the raft. As he landed, I heaved against the pole. By the time Rencevin clambered to his feet, we had been caught by the current and were halfway across the water.

For a moment I thought the thief-taker was going to throw himself into the water in pursuit. Then he leaned back, sheathing his saber. He set the golden monocle in his eye, gazing out after us.

Barnaby stood on the edge of the raft, staring back. As we floated on toward the dark shadows of the bayou, he called out to the diminishing shore: "Next time you see me, Rencevin, I'll be presenting the chalice to Queen Serafine! And that's the real truth!"

Chapter 9

I breathed in deeply, relishing the fragrance of the hot-leaf blooms. The flowers twinkled in the dark canopy above, sending occasional drifts of brilliant-orange pollen to skim the surface of the water. The hum of magic sizzled through me. I felt as if each push on the pole might send the raft hurtling seven leagues forward along the narrow waterways that twisted through the Mistveil Bayou.

It wasn't Bogthistle Mire, but it was the Bottomlands. There were no safe little Uplander stone fences and proper green hedgerows. Here there was riotous, colorful life, smashing its way out in every direction. Bullfrogs droned, alligators bellowed, peepers piped sweetly, and leaves muttered secrets to the wind. Of course, there was also Barnaby's persistent slapping.

"Pretty, she says," Barnaby was muttering. "Pretty

stinking miserable." He batted at his forearms. This merely displaced the cloud of needlewings humming around him, sending them to settle on his forehead and neck instead. "Ugh! How can you stand it, Prunella? This humming alone is driving me out of my skull."

"I don't need to stand it," I reminded him. "I was sensible and found a bladderwort." I prodded the bulbous purplish-green root that lay in one corner of the raft. "There's still some left, you know."

"I'll throw myself in the pits first," Barnaby said. "That thing stinks worse than rotten eel. I'm not smearing it all over my skin. I'd look like a purple-spotted mushroom."

"You'll be a red-spotted mushroom soon enough without it."

Barnaby was too busy whacking at the needlewings to pay any heed. I shrugged and turned my attention back to the map.

We'd navigated our way past several dangers already. The Hissing Pit, the Den of Wyrms, and the Bog of Sightless Eyes had all been easily avoided, thanks to the landmarks laid out on the map. We had nearly headed into one particularly peaceful, inviting pond before Barnaby rubbed away a charcoal smudge and discovered that it was not the Pool of Rest, but rather the Pool of Restless Spirits.

"It looks like we're about halfway there, if this map is to scale," I said. "We've just got to pass the Toll-Taker, skirt around this salamander nest, and then there's— Ooh! We'll stop there for the night. That will be perfect!"

"I'm not sleeping with a bunch of flaming lizards," said Barnaby, still slapping.

"No, not in the nest, that would be stupendously dangerous. But once we get past that, there's a firefly on the map. It must be a light-dell. Oh, you'll love it, Barnaby. It will make up for all this, I promise."

"More bugs," Barnaby grumbled. "I can't wait. What sort of forsaken slime do I have to smear all over myself to keep *them* away?"

"Bladderwort sap is perfectly safe," I said, brandishing the fleshy root. "And it's fire—"

"What by all the sweet hills is that?" interrupted Barnaby, pointing ahead.

The raft drifted out from the shadows of the trees into an open slough choked with gray-green grasses. The only channel ended at a hummock heaped high with burning branches. Billows of smoke filled the sky. But, impressive as this was, I didn't think Barnaby was talking about the bonfire. Something else drifted before the pyre, something misty and translucent. A shiver snaked down my back as I realized I could see the flames right through the creature, turned an otherworldly silver.

"That, I presume, is the Toll-Taker." Gripping the pole more tightly, I punted us forward.

The ghost wore a sort of peaked cap with flaps that hung past his shoulders, like the ears of a bloodhound. In one clawlike hand he held a shepherd's crook. Shreds of fog clouded his nondescript clothing. He batted away an obscuring haze to squint at us. Then he grinned. It did not improve his appearance.

"Been a time since Skillimug has had travelers pass by. Pay me your toll, then, and go on. If you dare." He snickered.

Barnaby peered past the bonfire at the rustling hedge beyond. "We could go round," he whispered. "It's just grass."

"Aye, boy, go on and try," said Skillimug. "You're a slithery one yourself, but you won't out-slither my eelgrass."

"We'll see about that." Barnaby tightened his jaw. Taking up the pole, he pushed us closer to a stand of the greenery.

The fringe bobbed suddenly toward the raft, hissing and twisting. Barnaby jerked the pole up to block the dozens of writhing blades, each tipped by a tiny fanged mouth. Gray-green stalks curled around the wooden shaft as he beat them back. "Auugh! Get off!" Barnaby pulled free from the eelgrass, then scrambled to join me in the middle of the raft.

"The toll it is," he said, still keeping an eye on the eelgrass. He dug in his pockets for a moment, then held out a handful of gold coins. "Not like there's anything else to spend it on in this stinking place."

Skillimug gave a gargle. "You think that dross is worth anything here?"

"Hey, now, these are pure gold! Pure as sunshine," retorted Barnaby. "A Bagby knows his coin, if nothing else."

"Gold does not burn. Gold does not fill the hollow places or the lonely hours."

Leaving Barnaby muttering a number of horribly unpleasant things, I stepped forward to address the ghost myself. "What've other people paid?"

The ghost clasped the crooked staff against himself as he hovered before the bonfire. "The Dark Lord Synerus offered the Unopenable Tome. Lazeera the Hierophant brought an albino peacock. The Wizards of the Black Sand offered up a cask of fine spiced rum." Skillimug smacked his lips. "Ah, now, *that* was a toll. The smoke tasted of cardamom and vanilla for five glorious years."

"So—books, food, drink, and . . . pets?" I wasn't sure which category the peacock fell under. As I squinted at the bonfire, my breath snagged in my throat. Some of what I had thought to be logs were something quite different. Bones of all shapes and sizes. More than just a peacock had burned in that blaze.

"The vigil is a lonely one," lamented Skillimug, sagging lower. "The endless hours, the empty bog. At least I have my eelgrass to sing to me." He swept out with the crooked staff, riffling the heads of the nearest grasses. I winced at the horrible hissing.

"Isn't there any other way around this blasted grass?" asked Barnaby.

"Not unless we want to spend two extra days tramping through the Mire of the Mouths-That-Walk. I think this is our best option. We just need to figure out what we have that he wants. Do you have any food?"

Barnaby unslung his pack. We knelt on either side, peering into the ominously empty interior. Barnaby stuck his hand in and came out with a single kernel of musty corn. He scowled. "I was counting on stocking up in Veil's Edge, but the blasted thief-taker tossed that plan right in the slop pail. I've got nothing. You?"

"We've got the map, but we need that." I tapped my lips thoughtfully. I had a few bits of twine, some snail shells I'd picked up outside Nagog. Nothing that would make a suitable toll. "What about"—I rooted through my pocket for a moment—"this?"

I held up Halbert's sketch of the bog-witch who had cursed him.

Skillimug recoiled. "Faugh! Do not show the face of that one here!"

"All right," I said hastily, shoving it into the pack. "You know her?" I said, after the ghost quieted down.

"I will not speak of her," he snapped. "Lord Blackthorn forbids it. She is the great darkness. She is the poison upon the land."

"I thought Blackthorn was the great darkness," said Barnaby.

"Pah. Nasty rumors. Foul tales, told by traitorous lips against the one who would stop the evils."

Barnaby looked at me, his brows raised.

I shrugged. "We can worry about that later. We still need to find something to pay the toll."

"What about that bladder-thing?" Barnaby said. "Maybe he needs something to keep off the ghosts of all the needlewings I've been slapping."

I jumped up. "Barnaby, you're brilliant!"

"I am?"

I marched to the front of the raft. "What if I go into the bonfire? Will you let Barnaby through?"

The ghost squinted so tightly I could no longer make out his pitted eyes. "Hrmm . . . A bog-witch could be good company, I wager. Do you know any ghost stories? Well, yes, then. That would be more than enough."

"Prunella," said Barnaby, "I am not letting you toss yourself into a blazing inferno!"

"It's more important that you get what we came for," I said. I leaned closer. "And trust me. It'll be all right. You'll see." I rolled my eyes at the ghost. I couldn't risk having him overhear my plan. If only Barnaby would understand.

Barnaby continued to scowl. Finally, he nodded.

I whirled around to confront Skillimug. "So we have a deal? You swear that if I jump onto that flaming pyre you'll open a way through the eelgrass?"

"I swear on the name that cannot be spoken, and by the third eye of Lord Blackthorn, the toll will be paid," said the ghost. He smiled, less fearsomely than before. "And it won't be terrible at all. Yes, the burning to death is unpleasant, but there are benefits to being a spirit. The sunrise in ethereal splendor! And the stars! And I will teach you how to control the eelgrass."

"Right," I said. Well, at least if my plan failed the prospects did not look quite so grim. Skillimug did not seem half as bad a fellow as he had when we first arrived. I almost felt sorry for what I was about to do.

I checked to be sure I was still well daubed in bladderwort sap. Taking a deep breath, I leapt into the bonfire.

It was blazing hot, that was certain. Bladderwort sap might be fireproof, but it didn't quench the heat all that well. I hissed, hopping about with my eyes slammed shut. I winced as things cracked under my feet, just as glad not to know if they were bones or branches. Smoke filled my nostrils. I could hear Barnaby shouting my name. I attempted a reassuring wave, hoping I was pointed in the right direction.

A grumble beside my ear made me jump. "And I thought the boy was the slippery one." Another grumble rattled my bones. "Out with you, then. You've bested me, witch girl. But I will hold to my word."

Something touched my arm, so cold it made me shiver, even amid the inferno. I followed the tug of icy fingers, to stumble out from the pyre at last and back onto the raft. I gulped mouthfuls of clean air, in between fits of coughing so strong I thought I might break in two.

Warm hands gripped my shoulders. I blinked the ash from my eyes to see Barnaby, milk-white and wide-eyed.

"You're not burned to a crisp," he said at last.

"Don't sound so disappointed." I coughed again.

"But how?"

"Bladderwort sap. I was trying to tell you earlier—it's fireproof. *And* it keeps away the needlewings."

"Handy stuff," he said, managing a weak smile. "Even if it does stink. I thought for a moment . . ." He shuddered. "Next time I'm blasted well bringing a barrel of spiced rum, even if I have to carry it myself. I never want to do that again."

"Fine with me," I said, surveying my singed clothing. At least none of the holes were in truly unfortunate places.

"Do you want to go through or not?" asked Skillimug.

Barnaby and I scrambled to our feet. The ghost hovered above a gap in the grass hedge that had not been there a moment ago. The channel of water ran onward through the gap, and into a dusky swampland.

Taking up the pole, Barnaby propelled us forward. Skillimug slumped, turning his back on us. He hung so low the hem of his ghostly robes dipped into the water, stirring up faint ripples. He let out a long, mournful sigh.

Barnaby caught me staring. "He would've happily toasted you to a crisp, Prunella. Don't feel sorry for him."

"I don't," I retorted. "Well, I do, just a little. He's lonely. He only wanted a friend."

"And a cask of spiced rum."

I waved away Barnaby's cynicism. "Friends are

important. I mean, not that I know much about them. But I wish . . ." Barnaby gave the raft another push forward. The grass edging the channel no longer snapped and hissed. I trailed my fingers through the rushes, thinking. "Barnaby, stop. Just for a moment, I promise."

Barnaby raised a dubious eyebrow, but obligingly jammed the pole into the silt, halting our progress. Seizing a handful of rushes, I set to work braiding them as my family had back home, all of us sitting around the hearth on chilly afternoons. A few moments later I had produced a simple manikin, the limbs and two plaits of rush-woven hair bound with my twine.

"Get on with you and leave me alone," the ghost called out sourly. "It's my lot in life."

I finished affixing two snail shells as eyes. It was the best I could do for now. "Skillimug, I have something for you," I said, moving to the back of the raft. Hefting the woven doll in my hand, I threw it toward the glowering flames.

A flash of golden light flared up as the manikin blazed. I caught a brief glimpse of Skillimug, mouth gaping. Then the eelgrass slithered, rustling back into place to close off the channel once more.

A hoot of laughter rose from the far side. "Well, sounds as if he liked it," said Barnaby, poling us forward once more.

"I hope so. I don't think he was really as bad as he made out."

"Maybe," said Barnaby. "But, filthy fens, this light-dell thing better be grander than the queen's drawing room to make up for that."

"It is," I promised.

The trunks of the cypress trees receded into shadows. Above, a ribbon of sky gleamed dusky silver between the leafy boughs. I turned the raft down a twisting water-way that wound through mossy humps of land. For reasons I couldn't quite explain, my heart had started to thrum. I wasn't scared, exactly. The light-dell should keep us safe from nearly any danger the Mistveil Bayou held. I stole a look at Barnaby, crouched at the front of the raft. He knelt on one knee, his chin raised, his hair brushed back, looking as fine and proud as the figure-head of a great ship setting out for the Palm Isles.

Something twisted inside my chest, like a bit of bramble tightening round my heart. I wanted, desper-ately, for Barnaby to understand the Bottomlands. I didn't expect he could ever love them. But he had to see they weren't all disgusting muck and danger. I gripped the pole more tightly, navigating a tight curve. The channel had become so narrow now that ferns brushed

the sides of the raft, adding a restless murmur t[
night.

We passed forward, under the arc of a root t[
spanned the channel like a fairy bridge. On the far sid[
the waters opened up into a round, limpid pool dot-
ted with lilies. I held the pole still, so that we simply
drifted, spinning out into the center. Above, stars glittered in dazzling patterns, hectically bright.

"Is this it?" asked Barnaby. "I'll admit the stars are
pretty, but I can see them just as clear from an open
field in the Uplands."

"Shh. Just wait."

We stood. I thought Barnaby must surely hear my
heart thundering now. What if the map was wrong?
Or, worse, what if I was wrong, and Barnaby hated
this, too?

Then a star fell from the heavens. Then another,
and another. The next moment, a shimmering ribbon
of light was weaving above the pool.

I heard the catch of Barnaby's breath as the air
around us grew thick with light. "It's . . . it's . . ." Barnaby gaped. "What are they doing?"

"Grandmother says they're dancing, telling the
ancient stories of the world. She told me sometimes you
can see things, in the light."

"What sorts of things?" Barnaby twisted around, nearly tripping over his own feet as he followed the spiraling cloud of fireflies.

"I don't know. I've never seen anything. Just twists and curls and filigrees like this. It does look like they're dancing, though, doesn't it?"

Barnaby caught my arm. "Look, Prunella. Over there. Am I seeing things? It looks like—"

"—a chalice," I finished.

"And there, that's a crown, don't you think?"

The spiky circlet fell across the glimmering goblet, and both melted away into a net of radiance that spilled across the sky.

We stood silent, too full of the moment to speak. After a time, the glimmering lights subsided. Drifting down, they alighted in the cups of the water lilies, turning the surface of the pool into a mirror of the sky.

Barnaby smiled. "You were right," he said. "This is beautiful."

We slept basked in the pulsing glow of the fireflies. Strangely, my dreams had not echoed the peace and beauty of the night. I woke early from a dream in which I had been carrying a golden chalice, holding it as tight as my dying breath. A crow had flown above, croaking

and screeching. Startled, I had let the chalice slip from my fingers to shatter upon the ground.

Barnaby still slept, curled on the other end of the raft. We had drifted up against the bank during the night. Quietly, I rose and crossed to the fern-clouded shore, then tethered the raft.

I set off after the scent of hot-leaf blooms. The trials ahead would be much easier to tackle after a cup of spicy tea. Finding a plentiful harvest, I filled my scarf with a half-dozen blooms. It was on my return trip that I stepped over a tiny pool captured between a turfy hummock and a moss-grown fallen cypress. In the still water, I caught a glimpse of wild black hair and pea-soup green.

I crouched down, peering at my reflection. The last time I'd met my own eyes looking back from a watery mirror had been the night I was attempting the wart curse. The night I met Barnaby. The night Grandmother cast me out.

Something flew over my head. A raucous screech split the air. I scuttled back as a large crow landed across from me. The bird studied me with a beady eye. A surge of hope throbbed through me.

"Grandmother?" I asked, finally working up the courage. The crow gave a chortling caw. Then, suddenly, the black feathers were shifting, the shape elongating, rising, whooshing up into a figure slightly smaller than myself. I gasped. "Ezzie?"

"Of course it's me," said my cousin, sniffing as she plunked herself down on a mossy hummock. "Did you really expect Grandmother to traipse all the way out here just to check up on the likes of you?"

"But . . . you were a crow. How . . . ?"

Ezzie preened, running her slim fingers back through the coils of her black hair. "Oh, that. Grandmother finished teaching me the crow-skin spell just after she threw you out. I was rather a quick study at it, if I do say so myself. I can hold the crow shape even in the Uplands, you know, as long as I don't go too far north."

"You've been following me all this time? Spying on me for Grandmother?"

"Hardly spying. I expect she only has me doing it for practice with the crow skin, and so she can laugh at the stories of just how pathetically low you've sunk."

Ezzie's prodigious nose jutted more triumphantly than ever from her narrow, pointed face. She had sprouted a new wart since I'd seen her last. Dark misery wrapped itself around me.

I tried to shake it off. Ezzie might not be my favorite person in the world, but she was a link to home, to the past, to all that I ached to be and see again. "How is everyone? Have Aunt Flywell's new spider-trap orchids bloomed yet?"

"Everyone's fine," Ezzie said lightly, smoothing the dozens of black feathers edging her dress. "The orchids are gorgeous, all sunset pink with little blue fringes. Auntie's very pleased. Though Cousin Elfreida made a great stink, saying they ate one of her hedgehogs. Auntie objected, of course, but I don't know . . . Those flowers are ravenous, and one of them had quite a lump in its trumpet. Auntie was going to duel Elf over it, but then Rosemallow came back, and everyone went into a tizzy over her new baby and forgot."

"New baby?" I wrapped my arms around my midsection, as if I could squeeze the homesickness back to manageable size. "I thought she was in the Palm Isles to restock the exotic-spices larder."

"She was. It turns out she met a sailor—a pirate, really—who fell in love with her. She didn't even have a seeming spell on. Anyway, she had all sorts of adventures. There was a kraken, and a typhoon, and a haunted ship." Ezzie sighed. "I hope when I'm old enough Grandmother lets me go. It sounds wonderfully exciting. We kept Rosie talking for ten nights straight. No one got anything done. And the baby's the cutest thing. She'll run to the beautiful side of the Bogthistle line, I wager. Not a single wart. Though that didn't mean much in your case. But still. Rosemallow said the pirate was quite handsome."

"What happened to him?" I asked. "Did he . . . ?"

"What do you suppose happened? Bogthistles may wander, but they always come home. Rosemallow said he wept when she told him she was leaving. I wouldn't have bothered. Take the babe and go, no scenes, no tears. But she's soft. She told Elf she even thought about staying with him." Ezzie grimaced. "But she came to her senses, and she's back now. He gave her a parrot, and it's the most horrid thing. Bites everyone except Rosie and the baby. It does have a brilliantly foul mouth, though. Maybe that's what you need, Pru. A bird to do your cursing for you."

"I can do fine on my own," I said, sniffing indignantly.

Ezzie stared at me. Her eyes still looked beady. "Right. Like the way you doused that woman with mud in the village that stank of eel? They were ready to toss you on the coals."

I goggled at her. "You saw that?" I managed to say. "And you didn't help?"

Ezzie shrugged. "You made the mess. It was yours to clean up. Oh, bother." She rolled her eyes. "I wouldn't have let them *burn* you. But you managed well enough with the frights. Even Grandmother said so."

"She did? What did she say?" I leaned forward, my heart thrumming.

"You know Grandmother. Hard to read as an old tombstone. But when I told her, she said, 'Any grand-daughter of mine ought to know how to deal with a pack of paltry frights.'"

"Hmph. I wouldn't call a wight paltry. And I've been doing plenty of other magic. You've just been flapping around spying on people."

"Oh, I've seen your 'other magic.' Good deeds. Feasts and cheering crowds. Prancing around the Uplands like you never set a toe in good, honest mud. Making eyes at some Upland boy!" The last she said in tones of utter disgust. "Really, Prunella. Do you even call yourself a bog-witch any longer?"

Each word hammered into me, but I clung to my anger. "I'd be happy to show you just how much of a bog-witch I am," I spat, flexing my fingers. "You can flit about the sky if you like, but I've got bigger plans afoot. I'm going to get Esmeralda's lost grimoire. And when I do, you'd better hope I don't catch even a glimpse of your tail feathers or you'll be cursed and double-cursed."

Ezzie snorted. "Oh, really? And how does dragging that boy into a light-dell figure into this master plan? As if an Uplander could ever understand bog-folk."

I gave a screech of outrage. "I'll curse you now,

then, you stinking little spy. You're nothing but a creeping, warty little toad," I shouted, jabbing my finger at Ezzie.

A gust of power whipped through me. Ezzie's eyes grew wide. A flash of green enveloped her as she raised her arms and launched herself up into the air.

The curse crackled beneath her, slamming instead into the figure that had just emerged from the ferns.

I could barely choke out one word. "Barnaby?"

Ezzie's flapping wings and croaking receded into the distance. I flung myself down beside the crumpled pile of purple velvet. I reached with trembling fingers, then snatched my hand back as something stirred within. Tentatively, I twitched aside the jacket.

I gasped. A warty green toad stared up at me.

Chapter 10

"Well, at least you won't be bothered by needlewings," I said as Barnaby flicked out his tongue to gulp down a mouthful of the pesky insects. "And you can still talk."

"That's like cutting off a man's nose and telling him he ought to be happy not to have to scratch it anymore," Barnaby said, his voice sounding tinny and strange coming from the small toad. I had never considered toads to be creatures capable of glaring in fury, but Barnaby was teaching me otherwise.

I didn't blame him. I had spent half the morning trying to undo the spell, with no success. Barnaby remained a toad, crouched miserably on the mossy stump beside the folded pile of purple velvet. How could I have been so stupid? "It could have been worse," I said, trying to keep our spirits up. "You're not a mudwhelp slug, for one thing. They stink worse than bladderwort sap. This way, you at least have hands."

"Hands? You call these hands?" Barnaby hopped up on his back legs, flailing his tiny bulbous fingers. "Oh, curse it all. We're never going to get the chalice back. How can I get us past Blackthorn's traps and locks like this?" He bounced into the air, nearly vibrating in his frustration. "You've got to try again. I think it started to work last time. Come on, Prunella. I know you can do it. If you cursed me, you ought to be able to uncurse me, right? I saw you break that featherweight charm back in Nagog."

"That was different. The wand was the conduit for the magic. The curse actually went through me. To break this, I'd have to . . ."

"I'm stuck this way until you die?"

I nodded.

Barnaby's pallid throat swelled and deflated. He blinked his side-slitted eyes. "What about that big magic book you're so keen to get from Blackthorn? That ought to have something in it to fix me, right?"

I sighed. "I don't think so. Esmeralda was known for cursing people, not curing them."

"It's just your sort of book, then." Barnaby leapt from the log, disappearing into a stand of ferns.

Even in that froggy voice, I could hear the accusation. "Where are you going?"

"We've still got a chalice to rescue," croaked Barnaby from somewhere in the greenery. "Just because I'm a blasted toad doesn't mean I'm not keeping my word."

He bounded back toward the raft. Miserable, I followed after him.

We navigated past a nest of giant spiders, slipped silently through the gargarou hunting grounds, and narrowly escaped a broody alligator almost as large as Yeg. At last the waterways grew sluggish and so clogged with mud and debris that we were forced to leave the raft and make our way on foot. Fortunately, the map indicated we were nearly to our destination.

I stopped. "We're here."

"Where?" Barnaby bounced, trying to jump above the screen of green rushes. "Blast it, I can't see anything!"

I caught him before he could jump again. "Stop croaking! What if there are guards?" I settled him on my shoulder. "There. Now can you see?"

Barnaby's throat swelled and deflated several times as we stared at our destination.

Blackthorn Manor rose from the Mistveil like the clawed hand of some enormous beast. Sharp towers pierced the thick mists coiling up from the sullen moat surrounding the manor.

"Well. I knew it wasn't going to be easy," Barnaby

said finally. "Go on, then. But slow. I'll keep an eye out for traps."

As we drew closer, I realized that what I had taken to be towers were not, in fact, constructions of stone or wood. The whole of Blackthorn Manor lay beneath a tapestry of thorny vines, twisted upon themselves to form elaborate peaks and prongs.

Windows glinted beneath the tangle, but I could make out nothing within. Though it was midday, the light was wan and pale, dulled by the curtains of mist.

We crept closer, aiming for what looked like a bridge across the moat. We paused in the shadow of a large fanglike stone. I squinted around the pale granite, trying to get a clear look at the bridge. Was that a gleam of torchlight?

No. It was eyes. Flaming eyes in bulbous orange heads. "Jacks!" I pressed myself back.

"How many?" Barnaby croaked.

"Too many. A dozen, at least."

"We'll have to go around," said Barnaby. "Maybe there's another way across."

"I hope so."

We crept along the edge of the moat for what felt like ages. "Prunella, look there," Barnaby said suddenly. "Is that a boat? Let's go."

I crept forward, still mindful of the jacks behind

us. We were nearly halfway round the manor, well out of sight, but I still couldn't help shooting backward glances.

Which is probably why I didn't see the pondswaggle.

"Villains! Intruders! Thieves! Bog-witch!" she shrilled, bounding up from the edge of the moat as we approached the coracle. "Who dares enter the demesne of Lord Blackthorn?"

Pale hair tufted above her greenish face. Her dress looked as if it had been patched together out of lily pads. A single pale-yellow lily was tucked behind one of her ears, in horrible contrast to the mouthful of vicious-looking teeth she bared at us. My breath caught.

"Well?" she demanded. "Have you come to steal my lord's treasures? To murder him most foully? To beg favors you don't deserve?"

"Actually," Barnaby said, from his position near my feet, "we're here with a message."

She scowled at us. "What message would a toad and a bog-witch have for the likes of Lord Blackthorn?"

What message indeed? I tried to say something, but it came out as a gasp.

Barnaby ignored me. "It's not for Lord Blackthorn. It's for you."

The pondswaggle blinked and pursed her lips. "For me? Who would send a message to me?"

"Your brother, Pogwobben."

"Pogboggen," I corrected, finally seeing where this was going.

"Right. Him. He sent us to invite you to visit him. He's got a new home, you see. Wants to show it off to his kinfolk."

The pondswaggle crossed her arms. "I'm not about to abandon my sworn duty to go visit some mud hole."

"Oh, it's much better than a mud hole," I said. "It's a pond. There's a spring, and rushes all around it. It's lovely. You really ought to see it."

The pondswaggle glared at me.

"Unless . . ." began Barnaby.

"Unless what?"

"Well, I mean, you've got a very nice moat here, but it's not quite the same as a pond. You're not a moat-swaggle, after all. So a person would understand if you didn't want to go and get your feelings hurt."

"My moat is better than a stinking pond any day," said the pondswaggle, snorting. But she'd uncrossed her arms. "I suppose it might be nice to see Pog again. But I can't leave the moat unguarded. Those jacks at the front aren't worth a sack of beans."

"We'll keep an eye on the moat," said Barnaby. "I'd hate for you to miss a visit with your brother. I haven't seen my own brothers in a long time, either."

"Really?" She beamed at Barnaby, rather a little too warmly, to judge by the way he suddenly croaked his throat clear.

"Well, go on. Don't worry. We'll keep things safe."

The pondswaggle hurried off. She returned a few minutes later with a large satchel slung over one shoulder and a pair of red boots on her feet. We waved her off with our best wishes for a nice visit.

"Not bad, if I do say so myself," said Barnaby. "Even for a toad."

"Poor Pogboggen," I said.

"I'll make it up to him someday. Let's get across. I think I see a door on the other side."

It was a door. A large oak door; very sturdy, very locked.

"You'll have to pick it," said Barnaby. "Unless you happen to know any lock-opening charms?"

"I could try a fireball. But Lord Blackthorn would probably notice that." I sighed. "I think we better do this your way." I grabbed Barnaby's purple jacket from the pack and found the picks hidden in the collar.

Barnaby hopped onto my sleeve as I knelt beside the door. Under his direction, I fit two of the picks into the lock, pressing one down while I sorted around with the other, trying to find the tumblers. It all seemed rather mysterious to me. It also gave me a crick in my neck.

"This isn't working," I said, fiddling with the stupid thing.

"It's your first time," Barnaby said. "You'll get it. Try again, lightly—don't bash at it. You're not killing a wasp."

"My hand is going to fall off. I say we just—"

Something clicked. With a grinding of stone against metal, the door opened. Barnaby hopped up onto my shoulder. "See? You did it."

We stepped into an echoing entryway dominated by an enormous staircase that curved upward into darkness. Barnaby surveyed the hallway. "We should check down here first. Try that room on the right."

"It's not exactly what I imagined," I whispered as we stepped into what had once been a gracious sitting room. Dust and webs had turned the chairs and lacquered screens into ghosts. Bits of dry grass littered the fireplace, scattered across a thick layer of bird-droppings.

"It doesn't seem like anyone's lived here for years," said Barnaby.

" 'Lived' probably isn't the right word."

"Do you think he's a wraith?" Barnaby asked.

"Hmm. Possibly. To have lasted two centuries, Lord Blackthorn certainly must have used some powerful spirit-enchantments. But people also say he's got three eyes." I shrugged, trying to ward off the fear fluttering along my spine.

We went down a dismal hall, then through a music room with a promising-looking collection of what turned out to be pepper-grinders arrayed across the harpsichord.

Barnaby spent several long minutes hopping across a pair of heavy wooden doors on the far side of the conservatory. He directed me to lift him up to examine every inch of the frame. He was heavy for a toad, and my arms trembled like an old woman's by the time I lowered him to the moth-eaten carpet. It had been worth it, though.

Barnaby spat out a mouthful of metal splinters. "Poison darts."

"At least we know there must be something valuable inside." I pushed the doors open.

Beneath the curtains of dust, gilded leather spines marched along the walls, shelf upon shelf. "The library," said Barnaby, hopping ahead of me across the shaggy green carpet. "D'you think your grimoire is in here?"

I raced along the walls, dipping down, standing on tiptoes, as I searched the titles. There were so many! The entire collection in the bookseller's shop in Withywatch would not have filled even a corner of this room.

A thousand and one books of power and mystery, but none was the one I sought. I was about to start a second search when an excited croak from Barnaby drew my attention to the collection of chairs ringing a low table at the center of the room. He was perched atop a large, colorful tome that lay open on a threadbare ottoman.

"What did you find?" I asked, my heart galloping away from me. I leaned over Barnaby, examining the book.

"Isn't it brilliant?"

I groaned. "We did not break into the manor of the most powerful wizard alive or undead to borrow his copy of *Lady Ainsley's Guide to Popular Fashion*!"

"But look at that jacket. That's a thing of beauty. Fellow like me would look flaming smart in that." He tapped his bulbous fingers against the page. "Come on, tear it out."

"Barnaby, you're a toad!"

"I won't be one forever. Let me have a bit of hope, now. After we return the chalice and I get my reward, I'm taking this straight to the nearest tailor."

"Toadliness aside, do you really want to be wearing an antique?"

"Antique? That's no antique. I saw the duke of Slayfell wearing one just like it to court not four months ago."

"Look at the year on the cover," I said, closing the book and turning it to face Barnaby.

"That's more than two centuries ago," he said.

"Like everything else in this manor, including the owner. Whom we do not want to meet. So we'd better get going."

I set the book down again. It fell open. Barnaby stuck out his foreleg, riffling through the pages. "I don't understand," he said. "Every one of these is something you'd see on the streets of Orlanna."

I held out my hand. "Do you want to unravel the mystery of Lady Ainsley, or find the Mirable Chalice?"

Barnaby grumbled something but hopped onto my palm. I set him on my shoulder, and we continued up the winding staircase. The velvety carpet muffled my footfalls. Distant creaks and groans kept my pulse racing. Every moment I expected to turn a corner and confront Lord Blackthorn himself, and probably a dozen jacks.

The thin light from the dusty windows lit a long hallway. At the far end stood a wooden door carved with thorny vines. More vines, real ones, had torn through the walls and crisscrossed the checked black-and-white marble floor.

"I think that's it!" I said. "Come on!"

I started forward, sure we didn't have much time. Blackthorn might already know we were here.

"Prunella!" shrilled Barnaby. Behind me, I heard a soft *thoomp*.

I stopped, one foot planted on a black marble tile, the other lifted in mid-step. Trying to maintain my balance, I craned my neck to look for Barnaby.

He lay splayed across the floor behind me, his bulbous fingertips jammed into the cracks between the tiles. I could just make out a distant, ominous hissing. "What is it?" I asked.

"Poison gas," croaked Barnaby. "Trapped floor. I think I've got them all plugged, but you better hurry."

"What should I do?"

"You should let the thief go first," he said. "But since you went ahead, we'll play the hand we're dealt. I'll keep this plugged until you're safe on the other side. Go on, step where you like. It's already triggered."

"I'm not leaving you here to get poisoned!" I said. "Maybe we can hold our breath and wait for the gas to dissipate?"

"That could take an hour. Unless you've got some flipping fantastic breath-holding charm, our best bet is for you to scram. Go on!"

"That's it! I can clear away the gas."

"I thought you said magic might get Lord Blackthorn's attention?"

"We'll deal with Lord Blackthorn when we need to. Get ready to hold your breath as soon as you leap clear."

Barnaby nodded. His pale throat belled out. I filled my own lungs, but I did not hold the breath long. As Barnaby launched himself from the trapped stone, I whistled, high and sharp.

A wraith of yellow mist spun up from the tiles, reaching toward us. The next moment, a gust of wind drove it back, tearing it apart. Somewhere in the distance, a door banged open. I hunched down as the gale whipped past. I pulled myself forward to shelter Barnaby as the tumult died to a gust, then to a breeze, and finally to utter stillness.

"We made it!" said Barnaby. "Better hurry. If that little hurricane didn't wake up Blackthorn, I don't know what would. But let me go first this time."

I jittered at the end of the hall while Barnaby examined the carved door. What could I do to stop Lord Blackthorn? The wind charm was good for a distraction, but it wouldn't hold off a host of jacks. If only I could curse properly . . .

"It's clear," said Barnaby, pulling me from my fears. Together, we passed into the room.

"It must be in here." I spun around, sweeping my gaze over the enormous amount of rubbish heaped about.

Barnaby goggled at the dozens of curio cabinets and armoires, each bursting with oddments. "What is this stuff?"

"Some of it's magical," I said, peering at what appeared to be a stuffed two-headed snake resting beside a collection of glimmering red stones. "The rest . . ." I shrugged. What did a person do with an oil lamp shaped like an alligator head?

"Over here," croaked Barnaby. "I found it!"

I rushed to join him in the relatively clear space near the center of the chamber. There, on a simple stone pedestal, stood the Mirable Chalice. I seized it, the gold cool against my hot fingers.

"Right, let's go!" said Barnaby. "Before Blackthorn finds us."

That was when I saw the dusty old lectern over in one corner. The aged wood was carved with thistles, and a single book lay upon it. It was only about the size of my two palms put together, yet it drew my gaze like the Northern Star on a cloudless night.

Esmeralda's grimoire. It must be.

This was the goal I'd been seeking for weeks. This was the book that could teach me every dark and dire secret that had festered in the mind of my ancestress. With it, I could be the greatest bog-witch of all. With it, I could go home.

Why wouldn't my feet move? I should be racing forward to take it up. For a true bog-witch, that grimoire was the greatest treasure in the land, worth far more than any golden chalice.

I swallowed the dryness from my throat. Barnaby was saying something, but the words fell distantly, like rain on a high stone roof. I took a single step toward the lectern.

"Prunella!" Barnaby croaked loud enough to set my name echoing back from the walls of the treasure room. I shook off my daze, turning to see what had provoked him.

A tall figure stood silhouetted by the torchlight. For one joyful moment I thought that it was Barnaby, that my curse had worn off. Then I saw the toad leaping toward me, fleeing before the newcomer.

"It's been a long time since any mortal has dared enter my domain," rattled a papery voice. "But I see you've made yourself at home. Well, then, let us have some introductions. I am Lord Blackthorn."

Chapter 11

Lord Blackthorn snapped his fingers. Two twiggy pumpkin-headed jacks stalked in and positioned themselves behind him, glowering at us.

"You will tell me who you are and why you have ignored my warnings." The man tilted back his head to reveal his face. Even the seeming spell on the mummers in Veil's Edge had not prepared me for what I saw there. It was the same leathery vagueness, with only a hint of color to shape the nose, the mouth. But the eyes . . . they were not black pools, pitiless and endless. They were something more horrible than that.

They were human. In fact, their hazel gleam reminded me of Barnaby's eyes. But I had never looked into Barnaby's face and seen such pain and despair.

"I knew you didn't really have three eyes," I said, telling myself to be brave. Or at least to look brave.

Lord Blackthorn gave a low, wheezy sigh. "I did. But I lost the third long ago. I have lost many things in my life." He squinted at me. "You have the look of a Bogthistle, I think."

I raised my chin. "Prunella Bogthistle." I raised the Mirable Chalice slightly. "And I'm here to end this thing's curse on the Uplands. You can threaten all you like, but it won't stop us—me, I mean."

"Us?"

I winced. I'd meant to try to keep him from noticing Barnaby. But Blackthorn was already peering down at the toad by my feet. "Ah yes. The boy from the Uplands. My jacks tell me you are quite the hero. Barnaby, is it?"

"I'm just doing what's right," he croaked.

"I suppose I should thank you," said Blackthorn. "It was you who brought the chalice back within my reach. What I don't understand is how you came by it. It has been tucked away safe and snug in Serafine's treasure house for two centuries."

Barnaby gulped and said nothing.

"Hmm . . ." mused Blackthorn. "You are rather well versed in locks and traps. You made it into this chamber handily, even in your current state." He laughed. "Somewhat mixed up, aren't you? The bog-witch making valiant proclamations, and the hero a warty, green thief?"

He looked back to me. "But why should one of Esmeralda's kin be chasing after that chalice? I thought your clan had turned away from the Uplands long ago." He glanced toward the lectern in the corner. "Are you certain you didn't come here for some other reason?"

I ignored his look. "I came here so we could return this stinking chalice to its rightful owner."

Blackthorn gave a rattling laugh. "Your grand-mother hasn't taught you very well, witchling. You do not understand the powers you are dealing with. But you will. And you will not like it." He set his gloved fists on his hips. His ragged cloak swept wide, swishing gray tatters across the floor.

Backing away, I searched the room for another way out. Barnaby hopped after me. Blast it! We were trapped. I raised my hand, my finger crooked. Lord Blackthorn was one of the greatest wizards of his time. I doubted I could do more than singe his eyelashes. But I would try, by the pits. I wasn't going to die cowering and afraid.

"I think you might be free of that curse in just a moment," I whispered to Barnaby. "Go for the door. I'll keep him distracted."

"Don't be stupid," said Barnaby, remaining by my feet. "You've got hands. You've got the chalice. You run. I'll distract him."

"How? You're a toad!"

Lord Blackthorn's painted mouth hinted at a smile. "You mistake my purpose," he said. "You may both leave at any time, freely and unharmed. But that"—he jabbed one finger at the Mirable Chalice—"stays here, safe, where it can cause no more harm."

"No more harm?" Barnaby said, goggling up at Blackthorn. "What about the curse? Until we return the chalice to the queen, things are just going to get worse."

"Yes, I am afraid they will get worse. But far better that than for the chalice to fall into her hands again. Serafine betrayed me, she betrayed all of us. It is time for her to pay."

I frowned. Clearly Lord Blackthorn's mind hadn't aged any better than his face. "That was more than two centuries ago," I said. "This is her great-great-great-and-so-on-granddaughter. *She* didn't betray you."

"Yes, she did. I am not the only one who has called upon my magics to sustain me these long years. She may parade about with that pretty face, but tear away her mask and you'll find a horror worse than mine." He tapped the spot on his face where a nose might be.

"You mean . . ." Barnaby said, haltingly. "You mean to say that's Serafine the Adamant herself, sitting on the peacock throne of Orlanna?" He shook his head.

"No, I remember there was a funeral for the old queen. Mam took us. There was a whole fleet of black-sailed boats. I threw a flower . . ."

"A fiction, to disguise the fetid truth. Serafine has much to hide."

"Such as?" I asked.

"Do you want to hear the truth? Will you listen to another side of the tale? You will not care for it, I think, if you've come here simply chasing glory."

I looked down to Barnaby. "Remember what Skillimug said? *She is the great darkness.* He must have been talking about Serafine."

He nodded. "We're willing to listen," he croaked, peering up at Blackthorn.

"Very good," he said. "But first . . ." Blackthorn looked again toward the lectern. "I am surprised you didn't take that, witchling. Don't you know what it is?"

"The grimoire of Esmeralda Bogthistle," I said.

"It is yours, if you wish," said Blackthorn. "I've only been minding it until the right person came along. The true heir of Esmeralda Bogthistle."

"Just minding it? But I thought—"

"That I stole it?" He shook his head. "Do you want it?"

I took a step toward the lectern, then stopped. My legs trembled, but I wasn't sure yet if they wanted to dash forward or run away. Halbert's face rose up in my mind, haunting me with his sightless eyes. Blinded by a curse. Did I truly want to have that power? Or worse? I shuddered.

If I opened that book, I would gain power, surely. I might even convince Grandmother to take me back. But I could see the person I would become. She had stood before me on the deck of the mummers' steamboat. I would be reviled, a figure of horror in little children's bedtime stories.

I wanted people to think better of me than that. It was a revoltingly unwitchly sentiment, but I didn't care anymore. I wrenched myself around. "Keep it. I don't want to be another Esmeralda. I don't want to curse people. I want to make things right."

"Fascinating." Blackthorn stared at me. Then he strode forward to pluck the grimoire up. He held it out to me. "Go on. I think you may be surprised by what you find."

Was this some sort of trick? I set down the Mirable Chalice behind me, away from Blackthorn and his minions, where Barnaby could keep an eye on it. Then I took the grimoire.

Near my feet, Barnaby's throat belled out with a series of agitated ribbits. Flipping the leather cover open, I bent my nose to the crabbed handwriting that filled the paper. Frowning, I paged forward.

"But . . . this is a spell to keep away wood mites. And this one's for soothing fevers. And this"—I squinted, not sure I was reading it properly—"'A Charm for the Proper Digestion of Beans'? I don't understand. This can't be Esmeralda's dark grimoire. There aren't any curses at all!"

"Well, there are a few. Old Ezzie always did have something of a temper, even in her better days. But that is, without a doubt, the grimoire of Esmeralda Bogthistle."

"How are you so sure? How did you even get it?"

"She threw it at me the day she ran away and hid herself in that bog and turned her back on everything else. I will explain." He held up his hands against my babble of questions. "But, first, there is something in that grimoire you might find useful." Blackthorn nodded down at Barnaby. "If you truly wish to set things right."

I hastily flipped forward through the spells. There! "For the Release of a Charmed Form," read the inscription at the top of the page.

I crouched down and opened the book beside Barnaby. "This is it! I can break the curse. You'll be a person again."

Barnaby looked offended. "I'm still a person. I just don't want to be warty and green."

"Oh, and it's so easy." I sketched the gestures the grimoire described over Barnaby's squat form. "There's that, and now I just need to . . . oh." I sat back on my heels. "But that's ridiculous. That's not a proper spell."

"What?" croaked Barnaby. "You don't need to smear me in bladderwort sap, do you?" He peered at the book, then sputtered with froggy laughter. "That's it? You have to kiss me? That's the rest of the spell?"

"I am *not* kissing you!"

He hopped onto my knee. "Come on, Prunella, pucker up. You did this to me, you undo it. It's just a kiss."

Well, then. If that's how he felt, fine. I would do it. I leaned down and pressed my lips to the top of his bumpy head, closing my eyes. The grimoire did not specify where the kiss had to be administered.

A flare of warmth radiated from that single, slight touch. A gentle *whump* of displaced air fluttered against my skin. Something tickled my nose. I opened my eyes to find myself kissing Barnaby on the forehead.

I scuttled backward, slamming my eyes shut.

"It worked!" Barnaby called out, as jubilant as a crow at dawn. Then he gave a strangled yelp and crouched over, apparently realizing the same thing I had a moment earlier. "My clothes!"

I was already digging through the pack. Well, it served him right. I chucked the jacket, hat, shirt, and breeches back over my shoulder. "Here. Dandy yourself up." I pretended to search for Barnaby's boots and socks until I heard him clear his throat. Then I turned back around, looking at a distant point on the far wall and trying not to blush. Barnaby busied himself brushing off his cap. He perched it on his head and gave a sort of sigh.

Our host had gone to the far end of the room and was speaking to his jacks. "Now will you tell us this so-called truth?"

Blackthorn inclined his head. He snapped his fingers, sending one of the jacks marching forward to collect the pack. The other approached me, reaching out ropy fingers for the Mirable Chalice. I snatched up the goblet, backing away. The jack turned its pumpkin head toward its master.

"Very well," Blackthorn said, dismissing the creature. "Keep it for now, witchling. Once you have heard the truth, you will be the first to set it right back where you found it. But it is a long story, and you mortal folk must thirst and hunger. Even though my home has few comforts, there are rooms more pleasant than this, and food and drink to be shared."

He led us along a series of dark corridors to another room full of decayed majesty and spiky vines. At least here there was a fire in the hearth, and a platter of tea and toast. I plopped myself into one of the dusty velvet chairs beside the tea table. Barnaby settled in the other.

Lord Blackthorn did not sit. Instead, he paced back and forth before the fire, pausing occasionally to look up at the portrait hanging above the mantel.

"That's her, isn't it?" Barnaby said.

Blackthorn nodded. He stared at the beautiful woman in the portrait so intensely it seemed his eyes might set fire to it. "The legendary queen. You've heard stories, I am sure, of her valor, and how she used the Mirable Chalice to avert the doom that came to Orlanna?"

"Yes," said Barnaby, taking the cup of milky hot-leaf I offered. "Everyone in the Uplands hears that tale on their mam's knee, growing up. All the dark frights of the bog rose up and would've destroyed the Uplands, but Serafine the Adamant banished them and drove the evils back into the Bottomlands, where they belong." He glanced at me. "I mean, that's what the stories say."

I snorted. "They leave out the part where Esmeralda was the one who did the real work until that jealous snake Serafine turned on her. They also say you're the villain behind the uprising in the first place." I held a cup out to Blackthorn. "Is it true?"

Blackthorn pulled his eyes from the portrait. "No." He waved away both the tea and the question. I sipped it myself and tucked my legs up under me, settling more comfortably into the chair. Our host didn't seem inclined to murder us at the moment, and I wasn't going to waste an opportunity for a cup of hot-leaf and a rest. "So what's your version?"

Blackthorn shook his head. "Even now I wonder how much she concealed, how deep her treachery ran. When she came to me for help, telling of a terrible force rising from the bogs, I believed her. I had seen the wights stalking the lands. I had heard of the lost, the harrowed, the taken. I wanted to save my people from suffering."

He gave a shaky laugh. "*My people.* Yes, that is what they were, back then." He stared again at the painting. "But, whatever lies she told, Serafine spoke the truth when she promised she could keep the land safe from evil magics. In two hundred years, not a single ghoul or disembodied hand has crept farther than three miles into the Uplands."

"What did she do?" Barnaby asked. "If she stopped the frights from coming after the Uplanders, isn't that a good thing?" He sat forward in his chair. I munched a slice of toast. I still didn't trust Blackthorn, but I had a feeling I'd need my strength later. And the toast was delicious.

"Have you never wondered why the Uplands have no magic?" Blackthorn countered.

"We do have magic," insisted Barnaby. "The wards

in Nagog. And the well in Sweetwater. Proper enchantments, not like the wild stuff down here in the Bottomlands. They do good things, and they stay where you put them."

"Except when they fade away," I said. "Like they all have lately."

"'Drain' would be a more accurate word," said Blackthorn. "The truth is that the Uplands did have magic once, as much as the Bottomlands, pulsing through the fields and along the roads. Now that power is bound. And it was I who gave Serafine the means to bind it."

I nearly choked on my toast, understanding suddenly. "The Mirable Chalice." I breathed out in amazement, turning the golden goblet to catch the light.

"With the magic bound, the frights were exiled. Save for on the Thousandfold Night, when the swell of magic is strong enough to reach even the green hills and villages. The people of the Uplands had no more fear of frights. But they had lost much. A few enchantments remained, yes, but they were the last."

"No more enchantments doesn't seem too bad a price for not getting your spirit eaten," said Barnaby.

"Perhaps." Blackthorn shrugged. "But magic feeds more than just spells. There is magic in all creation. In art. In innovation. In change. The Uplands are safe, yes. Safe and unchanging."

"Remember the library, Barnaby," I said. "The book of fashions."

He nodded, though he did not look convinced.

I lifted the Mirable Chalice in my hands. The gold warmed my skin, humming like the beating wings of a moth. "You made this?" I searched Blackthorn's leathery features.

"To my shame. Serafine said she needed the power for only a short time, to drive back the doom. And I believed her." He lowered his eyes. "Esmeralda warned me not to. She never did trust Serafine. But I—I was weak." He was silent for a moment. "When I saw what Serafine had done, I went to Esmeralda, begging her help to stop the monster I had created. She was not pleased."

"Did she say, 'I told you so'?" asked Barnaby.

"And worse."

"But did she *do* anything?" I asked. "The way my grandmother tells it, Esmeralda tried to stop the doom, but Serafine was jealous and wanted the people to love her alone."

"That is true. Esmeralda did fight against the uprising, protecting people from the frights with her not-inconsiderable magics. When she discovered what the queen had done, she flew into a rage. She said Serafine was a greater doom than any fright. And when the queen would not relinquish the chalice, Esmeralda and I made one last attempt to stop her."

"You tried to kill Serafine?" Barnaby asked.

"No. Death would not have been enough. We sought to cut off her magic. It was a brave and bold gambit, but it failed." He sighed. "That was when Serafine discovered how to use her greatest power."

"The magic in the chalice, you mean?" I said.

Blackthorn shook his head. "Fear. With her beautiful face and her cruel heart, she turned the people against Esmeralda and me. They believed us villains, kin to the very evils we had stood against. They even tried to burn Esmeralda. I think it broke her heart. People she had struggled so hard to help, people she had cured of colds, children she had brought into the world, all slavering after her like a pack of rabid hounds. I tried to convince her to stay, to have hope. That was when she threw the grimoire at me. 'I've no more need of such magics,' she said. 'They have turned from me, so I will turn from them.'

"And so we retreated to our own domains, where magic still flowed untrammeled and wild. In time, we became nothing more than the villains of mummeries and songs."

"All right," said Barnaby. "It makes a good story so far. But I still don't follow what's causing the curse.

Why is everything going bad now, ever since I"—he swallowed, then finished the question—"stole the Mirable Chalice?"

"That is Serafine. In order to preserve her life, her strength, her beauty, she needs magic. The chalice has fed her these two centuries. Now that she is denied it, she takes what's left."

"She's draining away the enchantments," I said. "But what happens when it's all used up? Will she try to steal the magic in the Bottomlands?"

"I expect she has tried. But there is another source of magic closer to hand."

My throat tightened. "The people. The ones who are getting sick."

"Hold on," Barnaby said. "I thought all the magic was gone."

"There is always magic in people," said Blackthorn. "Though rarely is it enough to be noticed. But there are those who have it more strongly. Those who could be witches or wizards. The chalice dampens their power, but it cannot stamp it out."

"Even so," Barnaby said, "how can losing a little magic make someone sick? It's not as if Uplanders are running around trying to cast spells and charms."

"Aren't they? Have you never seen a wheelwright

who does her job so well the wheel never breaks, not if it jolts over a hundred rocks?"

"Or a tailor who could create something like this?" I said, tapping the star-shaped buttons of my pea-green jacket. "Mary Morland. Halbert. All those others wasting away. The chalice stopped them from becoming wizards, and now Serafine is draining them away to nothing. That's what's making them sick."

"Filthy fens, that hag is going to pay for this," burst out Barnaby. "Sucking the life from the people who look to her to keep them safe. And they don't even know it's her. She's got them all convinced it's folks like Prunella."

I choked suddenly, nearly spitting out my tea. I dug into the pack for the sketch Halbert had drawn. I held it up, staring. "This is her. Serafine the Adamant as she really is, not that pretty, enchanted face." I brandished the paper. "She's the hag who cursed Halbert. It *is* a peacock on the chain around her neck. The royal insignia."

"That is her true face," Blackthorn said. "I am surprised she would be so careless as to let a likeness be taken."

"She blinded the boy who drew it," I said. "And we've seen others sickening."

Blackthorn nodded. "In time she will take it all. The folk of the Uplands will know only blindness, lethargy, dullness. Eventually, there will be nothing left. And then, finally, she herself will waste away. And my work will be done."

"And you'll just sit back and let the Uplands suffer, all that time? Until every bit of spark is gone?"

"It is the only way."

"I don't believe it," said Barnaby, bounding up from his chair. "There must be another way. What if we destroy the chalice?"

Blackthorn shook his head. "That would only prolong the matter. It would flood the Uplands with magic. She would have to make efforts to regain it, but in the end she would only feast longer."

"Might give us time to try to kill her," said Barnaby.

"I fear even that may not stop Serafine," said Blackthorn. "She has spent the last two centuries fighting death."

I pulled out the grimoire and began paging through it. "What about that spell? The one you said Esmeralda tried, to cut off Serafine's connection to the magic. Here." I laid the book open, puzzling over the page of closely written text. "This looks like it."

"It failed for a reason," Blackthorn said. "Serafine was too powerful, and too tricksy. The spell could not hold her."

"What if we used the drawing?" I said. "You said it is her true face. That ought to make it stick." I read through the remainder of the enchantment, which involved a good two dozen alchemical components and at least a half-day of inscribing the runes and sigils necessary to— "Oh." I pursed my lips.

"What?" Barnaby asked.

"Well, the spell is complicated, so you can't just spout it off. You have to invest it in an object—Esmeralda talks about using a peacock feather. Anyway, in order to complete the enchantment, we'd need to be touching Serafine with the feather while I lay out the final components and finish the incantation." I sighed. "How are we ever going to get that close to the queen of all the Uplands? And even if we did, she's hardly going to stand still for very long if we're tickling her with a stinking feather."

"Does it have to be a feather?" Barnaby said. "We could use this." He pinged the rim of the Mirable Chalice. "If we offer it to her, she'll be quick enough to get it in her mitts again."

Energy hummed through me. "It could work. It'd be stupidly dangerous, of course, but it just might work!"

"I've survived plenty of stupidly dangerous things," said Barnaby, grinning. "And at least it gives the Uplands a fighting chance. Let's do it!"

"No," said Lord Blackthorn. "No. I will not risk the Mirable Chalice falling into her hands again. I will not tolerate it."

"Oh? I'll tell you what *I* won't tolerate," said Barnaby. "A tattered old geezer who's supposed to be some great wizard, who'd rather sit and stew in his juices while his old flame destroys the lands. You talk a lot, Blackthorn, but what've you done? Nothing, except to sit here waiting for two hundred years until I came along to steal the chalice for you."

He seized the goblet. "We're taking this thing and we're putting an end to that hag. You can help us, or you can get out of our way."

Blackthorn stood as if carved of stone.

I was flabbergasted, but when Barnaby turned to me, I jumped up to join him. "You said you were waiting for Esmeralda's heir," I told Blackthorn. "Well, here I am, and I'm going to finish what she started."

Blackthorn sagged. "You are indeed Esmeralda's heir, witchling," he said. "And, Barnaby, you may be a thief, but you are a truer hero than many who bear that title. A truer hero than I." He straightened his shoulders. "Go on, then. Follow your plan, dangerously stupid though it may be. I will not stop you."

"Stupidly dangerous," corrected Barnaby, winking at me. "It would be dangerously stupid only if we didn't know what we were in for."

"Do you?" Blackthorn wondered. "Do you understand that, in doing this, you will set yourself against the queen of the Uplands? You will cut off much of her power, yes. But you are unlikely to kill her. She will seek vengeance, sooner or later."

"Let her try," said Barnaby.

"If she does, we'll be ready for her," I said. "But that's getting ahead of ourselves. First I need to find jackalope fangs and armadillo whiskers and two dozen other ridiculously rare components. And it'll take at least a day to prepare the chalice. And then we need to get all the way back through the Mistveil and up to Orlanna."

"My stores can provide what materials you need," said Blackthorn. "And I will ensure you reach the Uplands safely. But my assistance must end there. I cannot leave my bayou without surrendering to the full ravages of time. I'm afraid you would gain little help from a pile of damp dust and a leather mask."

Masks, I repeated to myself, thoughtfully. "Barnaby, the Festival of Masks is coming up. You remember what the mummers said? They were going upriver, to perform in Orlanna. Maybe they would take us with them."

Barnaby nodded. "And the festival would be a perfect time to make a go at this. Lots of hubbub. First, though, I want a good square meal. Preferably something with fewer than six legs."

Chapter 12

Two days later, we stood on the banks of the Sangue again, watching the evening steamboats chugging away upriver toward Orlanna. The Mirable Chalice lay bound in Barnaby's spare shirt at the bottom of his pack, fully ensorcelled and ready to be turned against its former mistress. It would be his part to get the goblet into the queen's hands, under the guise of heroically returning the lost treasure. Then I would enact the final bit of the enchantment to let loose the spell to cut off Serafine's powers.

I muttered the invocation, stopping just before the last word. I was desperately afraid I would forget it. My fingers twitched, practicing the precise motions Blackthorn had taught me. The only sliver of my mind free from these concerns busied itself with images of what might happen if I failed. What if I lost control? I might hurt Barnaby, or, worse, allow Serafine to prance off merrily with all her powers restored.

"I don't see the mummers' boat," Barnaby said, squinting against the last of the sunlight. "But there's another dock around that bend. They might still be there. Come on."

I was glad Barnaby could remain so focused on our present situation. The enormity of what we were going to attempt dragged against my every step.

"Well, there's the boat," I said as we approached the second dock. "But I don't see the mummers anywhere." There wasn't a soul to be seen. The *Brilliante* was moored at the far end. The cabin windows were dark, and no smoke rose from its chimneys.

"Maybe they're out there," I suggested. Across the wide river was a large paddler. Every one of its four decks glittered with lamplight; the tinny melody of a calliope echoed from its broad windows.

"Shh!" Barnaby tugged me behind a clump of palmettos. He pointed along the shoreline to the farthest warehouse. A lone figure leaned against the door. "Looks like a guard," he whispered.

"Oh!" I stifled my gasp. "Do you think he's got the mummers?"

"Let's find out."

Barnaby led the way. We ducked down at the rear of the building.

"I suspected you of complicity with the Bagby boy, Milo Gullet," said a muffled voice from inside. "And now you've proved it. Did you really expect you could sneak off without me noticing, after I gave you strict instructions to remain in port?" I glanced at Barnaby. *Rencevin*. "That was an unwise move for a man with your reputation."

The words of the second speaker carried more clearly, like the tolling of a bell. "I value my reputation quite highly, sir. My troupe has an appointment to perform for the queen herself. You don't keep a lady like that waiting, now, do you?"

"I will keep the sun itself waiting if I must, but I will have the truth," snapped the thief-taker. The front door banged. "Let's go," growled Rencevin. "I've a report of a raft matching the one Bagby stole spotted downriver."

Barnaby and I backed into the shadows, barely breathing until the tramp of booted feet dulled into silence. Voices murmured inside the makeshift prison. It sounded like the entire Gullet family.

"We've got to get them out," said Barnaby. "Come on."

I watched the dusky lane nervously as Barnaby

approached the door. He gave it a light tap. "Hey in there, don't worry. We're going to get you out."

"Hello, there!" called the resonant voice. "Listen up, Gullets. It's just as I promised. A hero has come to save us!"

"But the door's locked," said a childish voice. One of the boys, I guessed.

"I don't know any lock-opening charms," I whispered. "I suppose I could check the grimoire . . ."

"No, I'll do it. Just . . . don't let them know. Say it was you."

I nodded. As Barnaby knelt beside the door, picks in hand, I began intoning the bean-digestion charm to cover his clicking and tapping.

"Aha!" Barnaby scrambled back from the door. "You can come out," he said more loudly. "It's safe. But we'd better get moving if we want to stay that way."

Milo came tumbling out, followed by two younger boys and the girl who had played Queen Serafine. The older woman who had been the bog-witch followed more gracefully.

"To the *Brilliante!*" said Milo, leading the way. The pack of us ran down the dock as quietly as we could.

On his long skinny legs, Milo outdistanced the rest of us, leaping the gap onto the deck of the *Brilliante* and disappearing at once below. A distant rumble thrummed up through the hull as I jumped aboard. Puffs of smoke rose from the chimneys. Slowly, the great paddles spun into motion. The brown-haired woman unhitched the moorings and tossed them ashore. Barnaby and I leapt across the widening gap.

"Excellent! Wondrous!" said Milo Gullet, thudding back up onto the deck. He beamed. "To think we've been rescued by Barnaby the Brave, the Curse-Killer, the Defender of Nagog." He turned to me. "And this must be his loyal companion, Prunella, potent and lovely as a lily of the bog."

I nearly choked. "No toadings," Barnaby whispered in my ear. Then he stepped forward to clasp the man's proffered hand. "Thank you, sir. We're in your debt. If it hadn't been for you and your family, that blasted thief-taker would have nabbed us for sure. I'm just sorry you got mixed up in all this trouble. Let's hope Rencevin doesn't notice the jailbreak for a good long while. He'll be after us soon enough."

"Bah. We mummers are born to trouble. Trouble makes for the best stories, of course. And, speaking of stories, we must hear yours. But first: the pleasantries. Milo Gullet at your service." The man swept a low bow. "Offering masks and mummery, music and mayhem, with the Gullet Waterborne Players. And, of course, swift getaways from pesky troubles. Our *Brilliante* here is as fast as she is bright."

Milo corralled the children into a ragged line before him. "This is Lisette." He tapped the head of the tall girl. She smiled shyly, ducking her head so that her two long brown braids slung forward to shield her face.

"Florian," continued Milo, patting the older of the boys, who nodded at me, eyes wide.

"And this little terror is Timothy." Milo clamped a hand on the shoulder of the smaller boy, who was engaged in stuffing an entire stick of licorice into his mouth.

"And last but not least, the queen of the *Brilliante*, and of my heart, the fair Miranda." Milo drew the older woman forward. She nodded to us, smiling. I searched her face for uncertainty or fear, but found only frank curiosity.

All at once the boys began speaking. "Say, is it true you rode a phantom stallion bareback, Barnaby?" asked Florian as Timothy garbled something about pond-swaggles that I couldn't make out around the licorice. The girl remained silent.

"Come on, Liss," said Florian. "You couldn't shut up about Barnaby the Brave, handsomest, cleverest, most wonderfulest boy in the Uplands. Where's your tongue now?"

"Don't crowd our guests with chatter," said Miranda. "Let's all get inside for a nice cup of hot-leaf and some ginger cake. We would be happy to have you join us, Barnaby, Prunella."

The inside of the boat was as vibrant as the exterior. We settled in a small room cluttered with bright costumes and glittering masks. Painted screens covered the walls, so that in one direction we looked out across snowcapped peaks and in the other we appeared to have wandered into an elaborate rose-garden with a view of a distant marble folly. Milo and Lisette unfolded a long table in the center of the room.

Miranda swept in and out of the room through the swinging half-door. Before long, a fresh pot of hot-leaf sat steaming on the table, surrounded by seven battered, mismatched mugs and a platter of dark ginger cake.

"Please, sit," said Miranda, offering me a stool. The rest of them took seats on two benches. I noted that Lisette made a point of offering Barnaby the only armchair. I sank onto my stool as if it were a treacherous bit of mire. Was I really sitting down for a cup of tea and some cake with a family of Uplanders? At their invitation?

My wariness must have shown on my face. "Oh," said Miranda, looking at me, "don't you care for ginger cake?"

"No, it's just . . . You folks really don't care that I'm a bog-witch from the Bottomlands?"

"Oh, piffle," said Milo. "We're mummers. We know very well that the face on the surface doesn't tell what lies beneath."

"But I *am* a bog-witch," I said.

"Well, and does that mean we shouldn't offer you a nice bit of cake?" said Miranda. "I expect even Esmeralda herself might take a slice if she were still walking this earth." She deposited a large piece before me.

"And besides, we've been gathering tales of your valorous quest for the past month, for our next show. People need stories of hope in dark times like these. And it does sound smashing, doesn't it?" Milo flung out his arms, deepening his voice theatrically. "Barnaby the Brave, savior of the Uplands! Prunella the Good Witch, lov—"

"Stop right there!" I interjected. "'Potent' is fine, but if I hear any more twaddle about lovely lilies, I'll throw myself into the depthless bog."

"There goes your plan for a crown of lilies, Liss," said Florian, elbowing his sister.

Milo raised his hands. "Perhaps we're getting ahead of ourselves. First we need to hear the true tale." He looked at us expectantly. "Have you recovered the Mirable Chalice? Is this blight upon the Uplands finally at an end?"

"The true tale," repeated Barnaby, glancing at me. I nodded, hoping mightily that our decision to trust the mummers wasn't going to sink us in the mire.

He told them the truth. Almost all of it.

Barnaby told them about our travels, the battle to save Nagog, the journey through the Mistveil Bayou, his time as a toad, and the revelations of Blackthorn. He did *not* tell them he'd stolen the chalice in the first place. As he brushed over awkward bits, Barnaby looked at me, his eyes sharp and pleading. I shrugged, but kept his secret.

When he had finished, we sat still and silent for a long moment.

Then Miranda took the teapot firmly in hand and poured out fresh cups for all of us. Milo sat back with a gusty breath, nearly toppling backward. The children stared with wide eyes.

"Well. It's not a proper tale unless it has some unexpected twists, I grant you that." He nodded to Miranda.

"It'll have to happen at the Festival of Masks," she said, tapping her fingers against the table. "If they're to have any hope of getting away afterward."

"What?" I said. "Do you mean you'll help us? You believe our story?"

"When you've heard as many tales as I have," said Milo, "you begin to be able to tell which ones are true. And we know more tales than just the Epic of Serafine." He grinned. "So, yes, we'll help you."

"You might get into a lot of trouble," said Barnaby. "You'd be working against the queen."

"We've no love for the queen," said Miranda sharply. "She had Milo locked away after we performed the Epic of Esmeralda a few years back. The despotic shrew didn't care for it, and after hearing your tale I can understand why. But to take a man away from his family, his children, for a full *year!*"

"I'm out now, and that's what matters," said Milo, squeezing Miranda's hand. "But someday we must put on a private showing of the epic. I think you'd appreciate it especially, Miss Prunella."

"I suppose that explains what's happened to the masks," said Florian, thoughtfully.

"They're enchanted, aren't they?" I asked.

Milo nodded. "Forty-seven masks, handed down in the Gullet family for ten generations. They've carried the Waterborne Players through famine and feast, upriver and down, to the palace of Orlanna and as far south as the Palm Islands, or so my great-grandmam claimed.

"Forty-seven faces: knights, dragons, wizards, witches, beggars, and bards. When you put one on, you weren't just wearing a mask. You breathed fire and spread your vast wings. Now I'm lucky if I get a gasp when I set off the flash powder."

Miranda nodded. "They just . . . sputtered out. They're still lovely things, but they're nothing more than leather and papier-mâché and glitter now. The jack didn't make it through the last show. We've only Esmeralda and the queen and Blackthorn left." She sighed.

"Will they work again?" asked Florian. "Once you stop what the queen's doing?"

"I don't know," I said. "I hope so. Things will change, that's for certain."

"Change is good," said Milo, downing the last of his hot-leaf. "Now, we need a plan. You have to get up close to Serafine without a lot of fuss. And it just so happens we're performing for her court during the Festival of Masks, or we will be if we can get there before that scoundrel Rencevin can raise the alarm. How would you two feel about becoming mummers for a night?"

Chapter 13

I looked at the mask dubiously, hefting it in my hands. The great green nose poked up from the tangle of black-and-gray braids. The eye sockets seemed to leer at me.

"Do you think Esmeralda really looked like this?" I asked.

Milo looked up from the piles of costuming he had scattered across half the cabin. "I doubt she was green. But my grandmam always told me the masks have personalities to match the originals. Esmeralda's mask is a tricksy, stubborn thing with a mind of its own."

"Just right for Prunella, then," said Barnaby from the far side of the room as he buckled on his breastplate.

I took a deep breath and slipped the bog-witch mask on. It settled against my face as close as a glove. I plucked a looking glass from the table and held it up.

It was not me. But it was. My heart banged painfully

against my chest. I could only stare at the reflection. Me. A bog-witch. With a proper nose and warts that looked so real I had to poke at them to remind myself it was a seeming spell. If only Grandmother could see me. If only it weren't just a mask.

After staring at my boggy splendor for several moments, I found my tongue. "Well, they certainly won't be able to tell who I am."

Milo had begun rooting through a large basket that appeared to contain nothing but painted plaster fruit. When he had reached the bottom, he absently juggled two pears and a lemon in one hand as he looked around the cabin. "A mask has magic," he said, crossing to investigate a large brass-bound chest. "Put it on and you can do all sorts of things you might not otherwise. Waltz into an audience with the queen carrying a basketful of magical doodads, for example. Take it off again and you can slip away into the crowd, no one the wiser. Ah, here it is!" Milo tossed the fruit aside and seized a handful of white-and-red fabric.

"Especially if they're all looking at me," said Barnaby. "And who wouldn't be?" He had finished buckling on the armor and now stood before a full-length mirror on the far side of the room, turning back and forth.

"That's the spirit. Here, lad, try this." Milo held out a

white velvet cape, lined in scarlet. "You certainly look the part. Right, then. I'd better go help Miranda with dinner. We'll need fortification for tonight." With that he swept away through the swinging doors, toward the smell of frying ham, which had begun to waft through the cabin.

Barnaby lifted his chin, sweeping back the cape the better to show off his gilt breastplate and shining sword. I could almost believe they were real metal, rather than painted wood and plaster.

"Shame I have to cover my face up," Barnaby said, grinning at me in the mirror.

"You'll be glad to be wearing a mask later," I said, pulling off my own. "Especially if Rencevin is there." I fiddled with the yarn hair. We had docked in Orlanna that morning. The Festival of Masks was to begin at sundown, in just a few hours. The thief-taker must have discovered the escape by now, but with any luck he was still on the river. Nevertheless, I worried.

"You ready for this?" Barnaby asked.

"I've been practicing. I know my lines."

"That's not what I meant."

I let out a long breath. "I know." I set the mask aside and began packing away Milo's mess with forced briskness. "But I'm not the one who set out to be a hero. Are *you* ready for this? People are going to think you cursed the queen. Or worse."

"Only the ones who don't know the truth," said Barnaby.

"And you don't mind?" I looked up, my hands full of plaster fruit. I fumbled as a pomegranate toppled toward the floor.

Barnaby caught it, coming up with a flashy smile, as bright and false as the sword on his belt. "It's the right thing to do. That's me. Barnaby Bagby. Doing the right thing." He helped me put away the fruit. Several moments passed in silence. I could hear Milo and Miranda singing together in the kitchen. The shouts and whoops of the children drifted in from the deck.

"You know—" I began, but Barnaby cut me off.

"D'you have everything you need for the spell?"

I nodded.

He pressed his lips together, no longer smiling. "Good. It won't be long now."

The performance was to be held in the Royal Gardens. Miranda led us there: the two boys, Barnaby, and me. Milo and Liss had gone earlier with a rented wagon full of props.

As we passed along the wide cobbled streets of Orlanna, I stared at the city unfolding before me. It was larger than I had imagined. On either side, buildings rose four or even five stories tall, wrapped round with the wrought-iron balconies of fine apartments. The ground floors held taverns and shops beneath brightly striped awnings.

Flowers bloomed in every corner: Vivid red and yellow trumpet vines dripped down from the balconies; brilliant pink creepers spilled from marble urns scattered about the squares. Many of the women wore lilies in their hair as they strolled between the shops or reclined under the few willow trees that provided occasional shade in a green square.

It was beautiful, I could not deny it. Yet it was the beauty of an old length of silk—still bright, still lovely, but worn thin. It felt as if it might tear any moment, revealing something foul beneath the tatters.

When I looked for it, I saw the signs of decay. Rust bloomed along the wrought iron, beneath the flowering vines. Patches marred the striped awnings. Was it all because of the stolen magic, locked away in the chalice?

At the amphitheater in the gardens, Milo and Lisette had already set up the props and screens upon the stage. The semicircle of marble seats stood half filled. The pavilion at the front, draped in green-and-blue silk and embroidered with peacocks, remained empty.

We hastened to join the others, donning our costumes,

practicing lines. I sorted through the oddments in my basket a dozen times, making certain I had everything I needed.

Then there was nothing to do but wait. I stood at the edge of the screen, sneaking looks out at the tiers of seats. There was still no sign of the queen. What if she did not come? All our plans would fail.

A croaking cry broke through my fretting. I looked sharply at the line of magnolias along the path that led to the theater. A single black shape sat hunched on the highest branch.

"Go home, Ezzie," I said, although she was too far away to hear it. That was all I needed.

I was about to go and chase her away when I heard Milo's call. "All up now. Her Majesty has arrived. Time for the show."

I didn't do half bad, really. I only stumbled three times. Once was when I skulked out onto the stage for the first time and got a look at the queen in her trailing feather-fringed gowns and glittering peacock mask, which revealed nothing of her face. Miranda had to poke me in the backside to get me started on my villainous monologue.

The mummery we performed was not exactly the Epic of Serafine. Milo had introduced it as a "modern adaptation, with a surprise ending sure to delight and amaze." I didn't expect Serafine to be delighted, but I certainly hoped she would be surprised.

The queen stiffened at the first significant departure from the standard story, in which I, as Esmeralda, managed to snatch the Mirable Chalice from the treasury of Serafine the Adamant and whisk it away. That was the second time I stumbled, fearing she would call a halt to the performance. But Milo's quick narration flung the story onward, introducing the unnamed but valiant hero who would restore the chalice to the queen.

As Barnaby strode onto the stage, the queen leaned back again. I groaned inwardly. This cursed mummery was taking too long. I wanted it to be over and done, to know if we had succeeded or failed.

Finally, after a series of heart-pounding (according to Milo) adventures, Barnaby and I stood facing each other at the very edge of the stage, directly before the queen. I made my last villainous speech, setting out the components for the severing spell as theatrically as possible, hoping Serafine would not recognize the preparation as true magic.

I traced the last rune, just in time to be slain horribly by the hero. That was when I stumbled the third and last time. The crow began cackling as I cowered away from Barnaby's wooden sword. I stood there stupidly for several long seconds after I should have collapsed in a defeated puddle.

The crowd cheered as Barnaby, in his hero's mask, turned to face Queen Serafine. This was it. I craned my neck to watch. The pent-up thrum of the spell pulsed against my skin.

"Queen Serafine," said Barnaby, speaking not to Liss in her white robes, but to the true Serafine, seated beneath the blue-and-green pavilion. "Long have I searched. Many dangers have I faced. But I return now to restore what was stolen." With a flourish, he held up the gleaming golden chalice for all to see.

An excited tremor passed through the audience. I could hear the conversations bubbling up on all sides:

"Is it real?"

"The Mirable Chalice returned?"

"Look! The queen."

Serafine rose, as quick as a serpent. Take it, I thought. Take it! The spell thundered in my ears.

"My queen!" called an unwelcome new voice. "Beware! That is no mummer! That is no hero!" Rencevin charged into the amphitheater, shouting "Bagby!" as he drew his saber.

Barnaby lifted his wooden sword, taking a step back. The queen raised one hand, quelling the thief-taker with a gesture. She spoke to Barnaby.

"Hero, we are grateful for the return of that which we treasure. We would look upon the true face of the one to whom we owe so much."

"I . . ." began Barnaby, taking another step back.

"He's a stinking thief," growled Rencevin. With a roar, he slashed at Barnaby.

I leapt to my feet. I didn't care if I was supposed to be the vanquished villain. We had gone beyond mummery now.

Barnaby blocked the blow. But though his sword might be shiny, it could not stand against real steel. It shattered, sending splinters of wood and plaster flying. Rencevin whipped his own blade around again, smashing it into the side of Barnaby's head.

I shrieked. The audience gasped. Barnaby reeled back, his once-proud hero's mask destroyed. He recovered, knocking the remnants of plaster from his face. He threw back his shoulders and confronted the crowd.

"You see," said Rencevin, his lips drawn back in a fierce grimace. "That, my queen, is Barnaby Bagby. A thief and a scoundrel, like all his kin. He's the one who stole the chalice in the first place, and now he seeks to return it and claim a rich reward. Do not believe him!"

"Yes," said Barnaby, raising his chin. "I am Barnaby Bagby. And I am, or was, a thief. I did take the chalice. But I don't want a reward!" He held out the

Mirable Chalice toward the queen. "I just want to end the curse!"

Serafine's fingers quivered. She wanted to take the chalice, I could see it in the way she stared at it, unable to turn away. "Rencevin?" she said in a voice chilly as a marble tomb.

The thief-taker frowned. "Beware, my queen. Something isn't right. The chalice . . ." He fingered the rim of his monocle.

I hovered at the edge of the stage. No one seemed to care that I hadn't stayed dead. Everyone was watching the queen now. This was taking too long. Rencevin was going to see that the chalice was ensorcelled.

"No!" I shouted, raising my hand and jabbing it at the goblet. "That chalice is mine! The power is mine!" I cackled for good measure.

Barnaby whirled to face me, his mouth open. Rencevin lifted his saber. I didn't care. It was the queen who mattered. If she believed I was a threat, even for a moment, it would be enough.

Serafine pushed back her mask, staring at me. Her beautiful, untrue lips curled as she lunged forward to seize the Mirable Chalice.

I held up Halbert's picture of the queen's true face. The final words of the severing spell burst from me like a host of angry bees. The magic swarmed into the air, clouding around Serafine as she clutched the goblet. My ears hummed, my body hummed, the world hummed around me as somewhere an old, old woman screamed.

The Mirable Chalice shattered.

Dimly I was aware of Rencevin shouting. Everyone was yelling. I blinked against the stinging wind. Tears blurred my vision. I pushed off the Esmeralda mask, rubbing my eyes, trying to make sense of the world. A fury of magic swirled through the amphitheater, centered on Serafine.

She saw me. Her withered lips shaped a word. It might have been "who" or "you." I tensed as she raised her arms, recognizing the patterns she was shaping. Serafine the Adamant was about to kill me, and the only charm I could remember was my alligator-spoor curse.

Nothing happened. Serafine shrieked. She clawed at the glimmering air. She hunched over, scrabbling as the enchantment ran from her like quicksilver.

"Not much fun to have no magic, is it?" I said.

"Esmeralda," she spat. "You'll pay for this."

"I expect I will, but not to you."

She was going to say something more, but the air had begun to clear. Faces swam out of the miasma. A blue-uniformed guard. A lord batting at the air with his feathered cap as if he could swat away the magic.

"The queen!" someone cried out. "She's been cursed."

Serafine lifted her hands, but not to curse me. She looked at them, shaking. She tore at her hair, pulling the frazzled wisps forward, staring at them. Then she backed away. Taking up her mask, she clamped it over her now ravaged face. In a raspy voice she called out, "Seize the witch! Seize the thief!"

A fit of coughing doubled her over. More blue-coated guards emerged from the fog. "Get the queen to safety," one shouted. "The rest of you, after the villains!"

I could see the magnolia trees now, and nearly all the tiers of the amphitheater. Rencevin was gone. The stage was deserted, but for the shattered remains of the hero mask. Terrible images flashed through my mind. Where was Barnaby?

Not here. That was clear enough. I ran.

Booted feet pounded after me. I ducked behind a large stand of palmettos, hoping I was headed in the right direction, and held my breath as my pursuers passed. I turned to continue, but a caw froze me among the spiky greenery.

"Ezzie?" I called.

The crow circled three times, then dived. As it plummeted to the earth, it lengthened, spreading and changing, until a tall, sharp-faced woman stood before me.

"Gr-grandmother," I stammered. "What are you doing here?"

She set her fists on her hips, staring at me. "After everything that you've done, Prunella, why do you suppose I'm here?" The wart on the tip of her nose shivered as her nostrils flared.

Was she going to curse me? Had I embarrassed her so terribly?

I would not grovel. I lifted my chin. "I know I've disappointed you, Grandmother. I know I will never be the bog-witch you'd like me to be. But I mean to be the bog-witch *I* want me to be. If you feel like cursing me, if you never want to see me again, fine." I blinked rapidly. The last thing I needed right then was to be a soppy dishrag.

That was when the miracle happened.

She smiled. A real smile. Better than the one she'd given Ezzie that time. It sent a flood of sunshine into my chest, unlocking something that had been bound up tight. I sighed.

"A bog-witch should never be what others expect her to be," said Grandmother. "If you've learned that, there just might be a place for you back in the bog."

"Re-really?" I was stammering again, but I didn't care.

"Must I repeat myself?" The smile was gone from

her lips now, but it still sparkled in her eyes. "You vanquished that hag Serafine. You recovered the lost grimoire. And even Ezzie had to admit your toading of the boy was well done. So, yes, we—I—want you to come back. To come home."

"Home." I'd be able to see the parrot, to feed Aunt Flywell's orchids, to go on mushroom sprees. To be all I'd ever wanted.

She drew herself up, a pillar of black silk and power. "I will have to cast the crow shape on you myself, but tomorrow I will begin teaching you the spell." She raised her hand, pointing at me.

A thrum of running feet turned both of us toward the palmettos. The next moment, Liss staggered out from behind them, panting.

"Prunella! Thank the sweet hills!" She caught sight of my grandmother and skittered back.

"It's all right, Liss," I said. "This is my grandmother. But what's wrong? Where is everyone else?"

"Captured!" she said. "Oh, please, come quickly. I'm afraid that thief-taker is going to brand Barnaby!"

All I could think of was Barnaby telling me about his father. *I'll die before I let anyone brand me.*

"Show me where they are."

"Prunella." Grandmother stood aloof. "I told you.

It is time to go home. Your work here is done. Let the Uplanders tend to their own affairs."

"I can't just abandon them!"

Grandmother stiffened. "You can and you will. I have much to teach you. There's no time for lollygagging around doing good deeds for those who won't even appreciate them."

My world spun. Liss, Grandmother, the trees, the sky, the specks of magic that still glinted as they settled back over the Uplands. I closed my eyes, slipping one hand into my jacket pocket to feel for Esmeralda's grimoire. I took a deep breath.

"I'm not going." I rushed to get it all out. "You said I should be what I want to be. You said I shouldn't be what others expect. Well, that includes you." I took another breath, then plunged onward. "I *want* to come back. I want to see Rosie and Elf and Aunt Flywell. I want to make you happy and learn everything I can. But I can't just abandon my friend." Grandmother raised a brow at the word, but allowed me to continue. "And now that the Mirable Chalice is shattered, the Uplands have magic again. They'll need help. I can't just walk away from them."

Grandmother glared down her warty nose at me. "Instead, you will walk away from me."

I crossed my arms, uncowed. "You're the one who threw me out and set Yeg on my tail."

Grandmother's lips twitched. "That was for your own good." Then she sighed. "Well, I suppose I can't fault you for knowing your own mind, Prunella."

"G-good-bye, Grandmother."

"There's no need to sniffle and drip over it," said Grandmother. "Do your work. Help the cursed Uplanders. But come and visit one of these days. Your cousins will be happy to see you. Well, perhaps not Ezzie."

"You'll let me visit?" I wiped my eyes.

"Have I not made it clear that you are, and always will be, a Bogthistle?"

I threw my arms around her. Just for a moment, of course. Grimelda Bogthistle might smile on rare occasions, but I knew I was risking a nasty cursing by daring to hug her. Especially in front of Liss.

Grandmother pulled away, brushing off her robes and looking into the bushes. "I'll be off, then." She turned, raising her arms. Black feathers riffled along her elbows. "I'm leaving you something to remember me by, Prunella. He's a bit hardheaded, but any Bogthistle worth her salt should be able to keep him in line."

"Him? What do you mean?"

The feathers rippled up across her shoulders. She

turned to look back at me, her dark eye diminishing, her nose sharpening into a black beak. "Whistle," she croaked, launching herself into the air. She circled three times, then winged away.

I turned to Liss. "Take me to Barnaby. Don't worry. We'll save them."

The first part was easy enough. Even a full troop of Queen's Guard will retreat quite snappily when you set a giant alligator on them. In a few moments, the entire street had emptied of blue-uniformed guards and curious onlookers. The Gullets, abandoned by their captors, backed away uncertainly as Yeg stalked past them, bits of tattered blue fabric fluttering from his teeth.

The family appeared unharmed. But my heart squeezed to a lump of coal at the sight of Barnaby. He knelt in the middle of the street, hands bound behind his back. Blood streamed from his nose.

Rencevin stood over Barnaby. Unlike the guards, he had held his ground, a saber in one hand, a red-tipped brand in the other.

"Let him go!" I shouted. I signaled to Yeg, who obligingly snapped his great wedge of a mouth.

"The Queen's Justice will be carried out." Rencevin kept a wary eye on the alligator but did not retreat.

"Call off your beast, bog-witch. Or the boy gets a blade rather than a brand."

Barnaby spat, then tossed back his head. "I'd rather be dead than branded."

"I can arrange that, thief," snarled Rencevin.

"No," I said. "Rencevin, your so-called queen is the real thief here. She's the one who's been stealing magic, draining lives away. She's the real curse upon the Uplands. Barnaby stopped her! He's a hero!"

"Well, I had some help," Barnaby said, trying to grin at me. It looked rather ghastly with the blood on his face.

Rencevin's saber wavered, but only for a moment. "No," he said. "Bagby is still a thief. He stole the chalice. He will pay the price!" He shoved the tip of the brand toward Barnaby's cheek.

"Y'know," said Barnaby, "I'm glad I'm a thief. I'm glad I stole that chalice so that hag can't suck on the magic of the Uplands any longer. And you know why else I'm glad I'm a thief?"

"Why, boy?" asked Rencevin, scowling.

"Because I know how to pick a lock behind my back." With that, Barnaby swung one arm around, smashing the empty manacles into the side of Rencevin's arm. The brand skittered away across the cobblestones, sparking madly.

Then Barnaby was at my side. Rencevin's gargle of

fury was drowned by Yeg's bellow. The alligator started forward, opening his massive jaws.

"No, Yeg," I commanded. "Leave him. He'd probably give you a bellyache. You can hunt in the river. We need to get out of the city."

So we did.

Chapter 14

"I should go," said Barnaby, pacing around the cabin. "Rencevin and the rest will be after me soon enough. I don't like having you lot mixed up in it. I'm the one who's a wanted criminal."

Miranda made a shushing noise and poured us each a fresh cup of hot-leaf. The rest of us sat around the table, the deck humming under our feet as we steamed south, away from Orlanna. There had been no pursuit as of yet. Or perhaps Yeg had driven them off.

"Have no fear," said Milo. "The Gullet Water-borne Players will spread the true tale throughout the Uplands. How the evil Serafine stole away the magic of the Uplands for herself, how she would have har-rowed us all if not for the valor of Barnaby the Brave and Prunella, the good witch of the bog. The people of the Uplands will know the truth."

"The truth won't make a very good story," said Barnaby fiercely. "I should have told you what I really was. You were putting your necks on the line for me, and I let you think I was some sort of white knight." He threw himself down into the chair.

"Oh, bosh," said Milo. "It's more important how you end the story than how you start it. Besides, we don't have a white-knight mask anymore." He gave a smile as broad and warm as the noon sky.

Barnaby relaxed under Milo's beaming grin. He even took a proper swig of his tea. "Thanks, Milo. Miranda. All you Gullets. You lot are as much heroes as Prunella or I. We couldn't have done it without you."

"And you know," said Liss, looking shyly toward Barnaby, "reformed villains make the best heroes."

I smothered a groan. Dark-shadowy-past Barnaby appeared to be even more appealing to her than heroic Barnaby.

"We'll have the show on the road in no time," said Milo. "I've just got to finish writing the last act, and we'll need to put together the costumes. I wager by next year every village in the Uplands will have heard the tale."

"Thank the sweet hills, the masks are back in working order," said Miranda. "We'll need them for the epic Milo has planned. Even the dragon."

"But we didn't fight a dragon," I protested.

"Not yet," said Milo. "Speaking of which, what are you two going to do next? I could use some more material. Off on more adventures, I hope?"

"Of course, you'd be welcome to stay here with us as long as you like," added Miranda.

The two boys cheered. Liss, starry-eyed, said, "Yes, please stay, Barnaby."

Barnaby looked across the table at me. "Well, I reckon I ought to see my brothers. I didn't leave things in such good shape, and if I've got Rencevin on my tail he'll be on to them, too. After that . . ." He drained his tea in one last gulp. "I figured I'd keep on doing this. Finding folks in trouble. The curse may be gone, but with magic loose in the Uplands, there's going to be a lot that needs looking after. Not that I expect to fix it all on my own, but I'll do what I can."

"On your own? What about Prunella?" asked Timothy.

"Prunella will be back in the Bottomlands," said Barnaby. "She's got what she came for."

Heat flooded my skin. I could have shaken myself. I'd been an idiot. I'd assumed he would want . . . that we would— Suddenly I could not bear to have them all looking at me. I rose from my seat. "I guess I have.

You'll have troubles enough without a bog-witch hanging about. The sooner I leave, the better." I hastened from the room without looking back.

The problem with a boat is that there's nowhere to escape to, if you truly want to be alone. I moved to the prow of the *Brilliante*, where cool fingers of wind slid along my scalp. I could just spy the bumps of Yeg's nostrils, floating innocently alongside the paddleboat. I wondered if he would carry me back to the bog.

No. I'd told Grandmother I had a reason to stay in the Uplands, and it wasn't Barnaby. It wasn't *only* Barnaby, I corrected myself ruthlessly. I had work to do. Magic was loose again in the Uplands. I could feel it humming around me. Not as strong as in the Bottomlands, but the dead dullness was gone. They would fear it, these Uplanders. They didn't know any better. But I could teach them. I could show them how to protect themselves from the dangers, how to see the beauties.

Now that I'd set my feet on this path, I knew it was the right one. I could feel the surety of it in my bones. Still . . . I had hoped I wouldn't be walking it alone. I had hoped—for the first time, really—to have a friend beside me. Leaning out from the railing, I watched the ripples flow past.

Someone came up beside me. "Liss told me," said Barnaby.

"Told you what? That she's madly in love with you?"

Barnaby coughed. "Ah. No. She told me about your grandmother coming to take you back. She told me you could have gone away, been a proper bog-witch. But you stayed to help me."

"Not just to help you," I said. "I have a mission. I'm going to teach these Uplanders that magic isn't something to be afraid of. That they don't need to haul off anyone who's strange and different and toss her on a bonfire. That there's beauty in the bogs, not just frights."

"So you *are* staying."

There was an edge to his voice I couldn't interpret, and, curse me, I was scared to look at him. "Don't worry," I said. "I won't be a tagalong and ruin your heroic style."

"There are more important things than heroic style," said Barnaby. "Like friendship. Bravery. Doing the right thing. And you know, I think I'd miss having you around, Prunella Bogthistle."

Our words were a shaky ladder; all I could do was climb, uncertain if I was about to surmount a glorious peak or fall and smash myself upon the rocks below.

"I've gotten . . . rather used to you, too, Barnaby." I risked a sidewise glance. He was smiling.

Barnaby stuck out his hand. "It's a deal, then.

We'll give old Milo a whole raft of adventures for his mummeries."

I gripped Barnaby's hand. Esmeralda's grimoire lay solid and full of promise in my coat pocket, pressed against my heart. The river spun past us in a glittering skein. Joy bubbled up inside me, as green and fresh as a fern-edged spring. I didn't even care that I had no warts. It didn't matter. In that moment, I was exactly who I wanted to be. And I was happy.